Tales from
Happy Valley

Also in this series of new writing from LinguaBooks

Belongings
The Coiner's Wife
A Parting Shot
No Means No
The Taste of Rain
Narrowboat Blues
The Legend of Sidora

Front cover: Hebden Bridge town centre
Rear cover: View over Happy Valley with Sowerby Bridge

Tales from Happy Valley

New fiction from Calderdale

Edited by Ann Claypole

LinguaBooks
www.linguabooks.com

Paperback edition: ISBN 978-1-911369-32-5
eBook edition: ISBN 978-1-911369-33-2

First edition

A CIP catalogue record for this book is available from the British Library.

The stories in this collection are works of fiction. Any resemblance to actual persons, living or dead, or actual events is purely coincidental.

Cover images © 2024 Maurice Claypole

LinguaBooks
Elsie Whiteley Innovation Centre
Hopwood Lane
Halifax HX1 5ER
www.linguabooks.com

We are, as a species, addicted to story. Even when the body goes to sleep, the mind stays up all night, telling itself stories.

— Jonathan Gottschall, *The Storytelling Animal*

Foreword

The Happy Valley of this collection is well-known to millions as the location for a gripping TV series of the same name. The rolling hills of West Yorkshire and the unique architecture of the towns and villages along the Calder Valley have captured the imagination of the whole nation through its fictional portrayal as the setting for a gritty police drama. But Calderdale is a real place and was known as Happy Valley long before its recent media incarnation. It is even referred to as such in the correspondence of Anne Lister of Shibden Hall, familiar to the television audience as Gentleman Jack.

This book is not a travelogue, but all stories within this collection are connected in some way, either through their content or their authors, with the real Calder Valley, so a word about our unique heritage seems appropriate here.

Windswept moors and drystone walls, towering terraced houses consisting of over- and underdwellings and the aftermath of a rich industrial heritage are features that make this area totally unique. Visitors flock to the cultural centres of Hebden Bridge and Todmorden, and those with an interest in history and literature can climb the cobbled streets of Heptonstall to discover the resting place of Sylvia Plath.

Also buried in Heptonstall is 'King' David Hartley, leader of the 18th Century gang known as the Yorkshire Coiners or Cragg Vale coiners after the Calderdale village of the same name. Two hostelries in nearby Mytholmroyd, Barbary's and

The Dusty Miller, also claim historical connections to the infamous Hartley gang.

Railway and canal history is alive here, too. Branwell Bronte was stationmaster at Luddendenfoot, and further along the valley, Sowerby Bridge connects the Rochdale Canal with the Calder and Hebble Navigation and is also home to the deepest canal lock in the country.

The stories in this book range from the personal to the mythical; they include hard, real-world observations and flights of pure fancy. The stories are as varied as our landscape and showcase the work of a range of authors from differing backgrounds, all of whom are current or former residents of Calderdale and who seek, through this book, to contribute to the cultural life of this, our Happy Valley.

Table of Contents

The Lock-keeper

by Alison Milner

In the cleft of a steep valley, where moisture veils the air and laces the hair of its inhabitants, lives a lockkeeper. It is a willowy strip of land, a border between a canal rippled only by light and a river breathing the rhythms of the sea. A hinterland reclaimed from marsh by the sweat of men scraping heavy spades, dripping salt and peat water.

These men of toil with their strange accents and migrant manners were distrusted, even despised, by the eighteenth-century local population. They watched wide-eyed from their hilltop villages as a straight water channel was hewn from the earth at the valley bottom and fortified by slabs of stone disembowelled from nearby quarries.

There were no names for the shadows that climbed slowly from the torn gash of the canal excavations. They were not Grindylow water spirits who lived in the pools which stare like glazed eyes from the moors on moonlit nights. They were unfamiliar and therefore frightening.

The entrepreneurs who financed the canal were not fearful; emboldened by the birth of the industrial revolution in Britain and the economic exploitation of early Empire. They smelt money, stale paper and print. Lurchers sniffing out their prey, hunting profit.

The flesh on 'King' David Hartley's hanged body had not yet fully rotted. The clippings from guineas, sharp fragments of precious gold, were tactile; real to those who dwelt close to the Coiners, unlike the banks with their ledgers of imaginary numbers.

"The calls of redshanks, snipes and godwits were memories by 1799. The warbling of the reedbeds long since silenced by the striking of iron, the splintering of stone."

The voice had spoken my thoughts, italic letters flowing in the damp air and shaping into words.

The owner of the voice is a small man with dark hair waving beyond his shoulders. He is wearing a tweed waistcoat, brown breeches and Wellington boots. Thick black hair curls from beneath the neckline of his checked shirt.

"Millstone grit. Northern grit. Hard, calloused, and porous like the split skin of the labourers who built this canal. There is a pitted beauty in it."

"When did the Rochdale canal open?" I ask because I'm not sure how to converse with this talkative stranger.

"By 1799 the stretch between Sowerby Bridge and Todmorden was already busy with barges. In 1804 the full thirty-three miles to Manchester was operational. A water cord of communication. Umbilical, it connected the remote towns and villages straggling West Yorkshire and Lancashire; birthed a new industrial landscape."

"Yes, the South Pennine Ring."

"The heart of a ring is always in its centre. A hole to see the stars through, to glimpse into other worlds. There are ninety-two locks on the canal. You could call me the lock-keeper."

"Do you work for the Canal & River Trust?"

"Not exactly, but I help out with the travelling boats, the turning of the mechanisms to open the sluice gates. I live in the lock-keeper's cottage."

The canal is clad in winter, monochrome grey. Through the rising mist steaming as if from subterranean cauldrons, I can see the stone building he is pointing at. Corner windows, separated only by a single mullion at ground and first floor level on both sides of its front elevation, give a view of the canal in both directions. An open wooden gate leads directly from the towpath across a small, fenced garden to an oak door.

A gaggle of grass-cropping geese saunter past us, their webbed feet an orange splash of abstract art on a charcoal canvas.

"Maybe these are the descendants of the wetland geese, who lived here before the valley basin was drained," I say.

"Perhaps. A survivor species, they've adapted well to human encroachment. There's far too many of them now to live off aquatic creatures and plants. The bread that people throw to them creates polluting algae in the canal, but it keeps them alive. You look cold. Come on, I'll make you a coffee."

The lock-keeper strides towards his house, and like a goose, I follow. He leads me through a narrow vestibule, cluttered with musty coats hanging in the gloom, into a meticulously clean, low-beamed living room. I'm conscious of my dirty boots and concerned I'll tramp rotting leaf mould across the floor.

"Flagstones, no need to remove muddy footwear. Sit by the fire."

The stranger's smile is missing several teeth, but it is friendly enough as he points to one of two rocking chairs.

The red glow of flame tongues fire-eating a log provide the only light in the room as the winter afternoon thickens outside the windows. The lock-keeper hands me a pretty porcelain cup, decorated with hand-painted flowers. My coffee is black and aromatic. His hot milk is white and frothy.

"Lost orchids," the lock-keeper brushes his fingertips along the rim of his cup. "The dense white blooms of the Bird's Nest, the yellow petal wings of the Butterfly and the green bulging buds of the Frog. All varieties once profuse in our valley, poisoned by industrial pollution."

"What wonderful names."

"The old names, adjectives more than nouns, sound like poetry," the lock-keeper's voice is wistful. "Mountain Everlasting, Moonwort, Toothwort, Twayblade, Bur-marigold, Wintergreen."

I can't bear the thought of such beauty fading from memory.

"Nature is reclaiming the soil; peat is colouring the becks effervescent amber again. I've seen the black glint of Pheasant's-eye plant, with its faerie goblets of wine-red flowers, in local woodland. Heard the bells of wild Lily of the Valley chiming sweet scent in spring air."

I can see my face reflected in the deep, dark wells of the lock-keeper's pupils. I swim in his watery blue eyes as he stares at me.

"I am the keeper of many secrets, a compendium of the wisdom of the world, sadly locked in this box."

He lifts a large wooden casket, carved with soft fruits and luscious flowers, onto the table. The large brass lock on its ornate front shines like the Midas sun in the firelight, and I have to avert my eyes from the glare.

"I think, now after many moons, it's time to share these secrets. I sense a symmetry of souls. There is a recognition and a reckoning."

"Secrets?"

I am aware of the darkness, a giant bird spreading its wings, feathers fanning, shadowing the canal.

"Yes," he sighs. "They are heavy, riverbed boulders. I am wary of disturbing them, of releasing a torrent of destruction, but I will reveal them. Unwrap them carefully."

His fingers tremble like thin branches in a brisk breeze as he pulls out a neck chain hidden beneath his waistcoat and unhooks a chunky golden key from it.

The key turns smoothly and silently in the lock and the box opens slowly. Inside are hundreds of small parcels, swaddled in purple and pink tissue paper, each tied with a silver ribbon.

The lock-keeper removes one parcel tentatively. He flinches as the tissue paper tears and a strip of white card uncurls like a snake. Letters gush into words, and words stream into sentences, a calligraphy of thought.

"Flowers teach us how to live, blossoming in the moment. Leaves teach us how to die, in blazing glory." He unwraps and reads another, "Death, like the sun, cannot be looked at steadily."

Silence spreads like an ink blot into the room. His eyes are in full flood now and a chill like escaping insects crawls over my skin. I move as fast as a startled hare and within seconds I'm on the towpath, my legs hurrying towards the streetlights of the town.

It is over a month before I venture onto the towpath again, on a bright winter's morning, the low sun projecting a transcendent light show across the canal. I feel foolish about my hasty exit from the lock-keeper's home now, and decide to saunter past with slow, deliberate steps. Its corner windows are shimmering opaque. A 'For Sale by Auction' sign in large, red capitals is nailed onto the fence.

"Offcumdens will bid and buy Black Pit Lock Cottage."

An old woman walking past stops beside me, shivers further into her woolly shawl, and laughs.

"They'll think it's a bargain, but they'll get more than they bargained for. Local folk know the lock-keeper's home comes with a household boggart. He's a helpful hob, but he needs to be tret right, or there will be trouble."

A Shot in the Park

By Chris Freeman

As I stopped, the car radio was playing Electric Dreams, an all-time favourite of mine. Leaving the ignition on I opened my door, reached round and took the bag off the back seat and went to put it in the boot.

Strange, but the passenger in the car facing me got out a moment after me, but as I went to the boot, he got back into the passenger seat. Probably forgotten something.

I was at the park to have a look at the possibility of doing some work for the park rangers; bird and bat boxes and maybe repair the benches. I would need photos, so I had my camera to hand.

At the top of the fairly steep driveway entering Shroggs Park, a man was standing on the edge of the grass, ahead and to my left. As I got nearer to him, he looked at me. I say looked at me, but it was more a stare past me; then I realised why. The man walking behind me, the passenger from the car, strode past me and raising his right hand loosed two rounds from and automatic pistol. I instinctively switched my camera on and took several consecutive pictures, shooting from the hip so as not to be seen taking them.

The man to my left then quite calmly said, "You've shot me in the chest."

The assailant then ran off deeper into the park and disappeared into the thicket of rhododendrons.

I quickly dialled 999 and waited what seemed an age to get through. When the operator finally answered, I related all of the incident to her and said that I would stay with the victim, but as he was still ambulatory, would remove him to a safer place, just in case the gunman returned. She told me to be careful and to stay on the phone until the police arrived.

Looking over the wall of the park, I noted that the black car, previously parked in front of my car, had gone, so I led the guy back down the sloping driveway.

He stopped, held out his hand, and said, "It's getting dark, can you hold my hand mate, I can't see the way."

Apparently, my hands-free phone was relaying all of this back to the ambulance crew who were speeding our way.

The guy was now beginning to bleed quite a lot from the hole in his upper right chest and from the flesh wound to his right shoulder. I grabbed the black bin liner I keep for kneeling on the ground to change a wheel and throwing that over the car seat, carefully sat him down. He looked awfully pale and his pulse was almost too weak to measure.

The air was filled with the sound of wailing sirens and within moments both police and ambulance arrived. The victim was removed to the ambulance and with an accompanying policeman, sped off to the hospital.

I was whisked off to the nearest police car. They wanted the SD memory card from my camera of course, so it was a good job that I had previously emptied the contents onto the computer and there were just the shots from the park.

You know how you sometimes get a light-bulb moment, well I did. It suddenly dawned on me that the dash cam, which would still have been recording because the radio was on, would have picked up the car and passenger parked in front of me. It would also have seen the face of the passenger, possibly the assailant.

"Better have the SD memory card from my dash cam too," I told the officer.

"Why?" he asked.

"Well," I said, "it might just have recorded your assailant, complete with Electric Dreams."

"Well," said the officer, "it's a shot in the dark, but if it is on there, that's brilliant. Thanks mate."

And the good news; The guy made a full recovery, and two men were arrested; one for attempted murder and the other as an accomplice. The guy who was shot doesn't sell drugs anymore and the other two can't, as they're locked up.

Mixed Signals

by Alison Milner

The vampires stir in the lamp room at Hebden Bridge railway station now the bats have moved out, in this second great age of the Gothic.

In the past, their savings sustained them, but they are vagrants now, tormented by enterprising schemes that pall in the intense light of modern technology.

The vampires joke that the lamp room wears shades less stylish than their own, shields shame at such ruin as weeds, like hair, tangle its roofline. They are sure the lamp room remembers its bright beacons shining; rays splitting the gloom on dark winter mornings as workers stack the platform, coughing soot amid the embers of dying dreams from tired lungs.

They like the oily blackness, and the irony of their abode amuses them. A small stone temple to light and nineteenth-century industry now blinded, eyes gouged, blinkered by black window shutters.

The disused signal box next door has friends and a 'Save It' leaflet to prove it, but the lamp room only has fiends, the vampires laugh. It is listed but not loved, warped by wet weather and the long reach of lichen. Its utility turned to futility in an instant by electricity.

It isn't easy for them to collect converts anymore the vampires muse as they shelter from the lengthening light of summer. Immortality is no longer regarded as a miracle. Death is now more desirable than artificially prolonged life. Social distancing habits are making their lifestyle much more difficult. Humans are wary of strangers. Scared of climate change and the collapse of civilisation in coming centuries. Frightened of future pandemics, just around the corner on a blind bend in time.

Avoiding the ghosts of the demolished cottages at the railway track side, the vampires sleep out the sun, smelling the strong scent of human, the iron tang of blood coursing veins.

The wind is whispering of winter and there is a ripening in the air. Apple globes hang heavy, worlds of metamorphosis for wingless insects. It is time for the tiring trek north, to the days of deep darkness. A fuelling frenzy is necessary.

Ralph is bored with this routine. He knows his name means wolf counsel, but vampires don't hunt in packs; becoming one hadn't been a wise transition for him. Lately he had been feeling that black wasn't his colour. Plenty of young men these days dress in pink. Perhaps red would be an acceptable compromise to his vampire cohort, only he hadn't worked out a way to conduct that conversation with them. Like many who have lived too long, their habits are fixed, their ideas inscribed in stone.

Crouched in blankets the vampires wait, until the daylight dissipates, until a pale moon with heavy-lidded eyes rises high in the night sky.

The vampires open their eyes when they sense the swooping of owls in heavy flight. There is a languid unwrapping of limbs as they uncurl, cast off their bedding and dress in smart sharp jackets. Timeless attire, costume theatre for the drama of the night to come. The clatter of a dozen discarded sunglasses on a stone shelf signals they are ready. Now the blistering, the biting of necks can begin. They shake hands solemnly, a ritual of respect before they assert the right to vanish individually into the cold, viscous night.

"My teeth have grown a bit blunt," Ralph says, taking a metal file from his pocket.

"I'll sharpen up before I leave."

The other vampires nod their acknowledgement, but without much interest.

"Make yourself useful while we're out," says one.

"Check the prices of snow goggles online. We may need them this year in the mountains. And the rate of inflation is killing."

The vampires are fearful of heavy snow, the sort that falls silently, stealthily. It isn't the walking. It is the searing brightness, slowing their relentless march to the vast flatlands of diluted light on the most northerly shore of Britain that troubles them.

"Actually, I was thinking of trying my luck on the early morning trains," Ralph says as the room empties.

At 5.15am he creases his body into one of the hard wooden benches on the deserted platform. The darkness is intensified in the inky pools of greasy water puckering like toothless mouths at his feet. It is damp, still, and silent. The moon displays a thin-lipped grin behind black cloud, gleaming like a clown's face paint.

He waits patiently for an early passenger to appear. With luck he'll have a quarter of an hour to establish an acquaintance and even secure a puncture, or at least the possibility of one, before the 5.45am to Leeds shuffles into the station.

Ralph hears the irregular rhythm of paws clicking on the paving stones before he sees the dog, skittering ungainly on three legs. Holding its lead is a young woman. Small and slim she props herself silently against the door of the locked waiting room. Her head is couched in a voluminous cloak.

"Miserable morning." Ralph speaks in a tone he hopes evokes empathy. The young woman swivels her head slowly.

"Well, I'm still standing. Could be the last one standing; our world is unravelling like a ribbon."

"Yes, it's all very worrying."

Ralph wonders if she is referring to the cost of living, climate change, lost love, or a tangle of all three.

The young woman emerges slowly from her hood like a reptile shedding skin. Her hair is short and spiky, her eyes are pale and sunken. Her tongue, illuminated by a flickering lighter, spits strands of tobacco.

"Mind if I smoke?"

"No, only advantage of sitting on a deserted platform at this time of day," says Ralph, turning his face from the spark.

The stranger is animated now, feet tapping to a tune audible only to herself.

"We should grasp the darting ribbon. Mark a trail for the threads of our futures. Plants can provide a solution to all problems, from cannabis to cabbage, beans to broccoli. Cereals could solve the woes of the world. Climate change can be reversed, pandemics eliminated forever, just by stopping eating meat and dairy products."

"What about blood?" Ralph says, confused by this ardent young woman who is obviously on a mission to convince and cajole very different to his own.

"Vitamin B12," she says as she sits down beside him, "found in some wholefoods, but you can take it in tablet form too."

He watches the skin on her neck gently moving, lapping like little waves, as she speaks. He notices she has a small tattoo just below her jaw on the left-hand side, two italic capital Vs like a child's drawing of birds flying.

She rummages in the deep pockets of her baggy trousers and pulls out a tatty paperback book. Ralph's initial disappointment that further opportunities for conversation might be curtailed dissipates when he reads the title, 'Old Norse Myths'. He might have more in common with the stranger than he'd initially thought. She obviously finds ancient stories from wild, cold places interesting, romantic even. Perhaps the book explains her obsession with preserving the world's ice.

"Valhalla's a vegan as well."

She places 'Old Norse Myths' unopened on the bench and points at the dog who is now curled asleep.

Privately he wonders if the dog's diet is responsible for its three legs, but thinks it impolite to ask.

23

"I'm Valerie," she says as she grasps his gloved hand with enthusiasm. "You could be vegan too."

He leans closer. He senses the pulse in her neck fluttering, as if the tattoo birds are starting to flap their wings. She is right, he could be. No more biting necessary, just the swallowing of pills, clean and clinical. He'd write a book, 'From Vampire to Vegan'. It would be a bestseller. He'd be famous, a celebrity. He wouldn't even have to face the bright lights of the television studios, he'd be a social media sensation.

Meat-free living could be the remedy for the endless stretch of his future; days of drizzle and discomfort without end. Maybe he'd gain a new energy, be able to resurrect an excitement for life which he hadn't felt for at least a century. He'd find new acquaintances, pulsing with life to replace his old vampire colleagues who had become tedious with their traditions.

He'd be able to move out of the lamp room into a proper home. There are several suitable stone houses he can see from the railway station, gothic and grey. Some with fancy turrets and ornate attic windows. Dwellings fit for princes of profit, built for Victorian mill owners.

"So what do vegans eat - nut roast?"

The girl looks at Ralph for a long time before she snorts with annoyance.

The pain is sudden and sharp, his carotid artery cut by a single deft slice of her knife. His throat gashes red like a slashed velvet lining in a dark wool coat.

V V – Vegan Vigilante, Vampire Vanguard, Valerie Valkyrie, whichever, they would all have their reasons, Ralph thinks as his blood pools like a liquid eye on the platform.

That morning, the 5.45 travelling east is cancelled due to an incident on the line.

The Big Story

by Roy Greenwood

Norman hurried into the office, eager to start work. It was still there today the enthusiasm he had felt those three months ago when he had first taken his place in the reporters' room as a very raw recruit.

Life as a weekly newspaper reporter in the 1960s had seemed very glamorous to 18-year-old Norman – for a week at least. Then he had begun to realise there was more to it than that and ever since it had been a matter of routine. But today it was different.

"Don't bother taking your coat off, Norman," came the voice from behind the half-open editor's door.

That was it, the call Norman had been hoping for. He pushed open the door and went in.

"What's up, Mr Bradley?" he asked, trying not to look too excited.

David Bradley looked up from his morning paper, crossed his fingers and said, "Have you seen this in the mornings about this miner? He lives in our area."

"Yes, I read it at home," replied Norman. "Do you want me to do the story?" he asked excitedly.

Bradley paused. There was no other way.

"Yes, you'd better get up there straight away. Joe's off and Jean'll be at court all day."

He briefed him carefully – the miner had been killed in an accident at a nearby pit. Bradley himself was handling the pit side, contacting Coal Board and union officials, Norman was to find out more about the man himself. He would be going to his home, speaking to relatives and neighbours.

As Norman was about to leave, Bradley looked up at him and wondered would he ever make a reporter – he hadn't shown many signs of it so far. But damn it all, he had to give the lad a chance.

"And, Norman," he called. Norman froze. "Don't muck it up. Do it well and you might even get your first by-line."

"Don't worry, Mr Bradley," he said cheerfully and shut the door.

As he walked down the stairs, he wondered why the thought of the tragedy excited him and why bad news was good news to a newspaperman.

But then he thought about the by-line. It would look good on the front page – 'By Norman Armstrong'. *Maybe I ought to change my name to something with a more of a ring to it when I join one of the nationals*, he thought.

However, the editor's voice from upstairs broke his dream.

"Is Albert in yet?"

Albert was the paper's sub-editor and had worked for the firm for 35 years. He was guaranteed to know everyone and everything in the town.

"No, Mr Bradley, he hasn't arrived yet," shouted Norman.

"Well, you'd better get off and check with him when you get back" came the reply.

The miner's name had been given by the morning paper as George Littlewood, aged 42, of 11 Victoria Terrace on the outskirts of the town. It was not difficult for Norman to find – it was the only row still standing, like a dilapidated island in a sea of cleared homes.

He looked at the row of houses, very few seemed occupied, so he went directly to number 11.

He knocked and waited – no answer. He looked through the window but could see little other than an old fashioned fireplace with a few ornaments on the mantelpiece and a faded brown settee.

He was just about to turn away, but decided to try the door. Gingerly he turned the handle and to his surprise the door opened. He looked up and down the street and then slowly stepped through into the house.

Norman found himself in a rather dark hallway and looked through a door into a dingy living room. As he started to make his way in, there was a bang and the outer door slammed shut behind him.

Startled, he swung round. Slowly he turned back and was startled again to see a man standing in the corner of the living room.

"Well, lad, what dost tha want?" the man asked.

A little shaken, Norman stood there looking at him. The man seemed as if he had just come up from the pit himself. He was wearing an old fashioned, dirty grey suit with a very dirty shirt and no tie. He looked to be in his early forties.

Slowly he brushed his right hand through his dishevelled hair and Norman noticed a strange thing. The man was missing two fingers from his hand.

"Well, lad?" he asked again.

"Oh…er I'm from the Chronicle," Norman finally manged to say in a small voice.

"Ah s'pose tha's come about our George," said the man.

"Yes," answered Norman hesitantly.

"Ah tried to warn him tha knows," said the man. "Ah tried t'tell 'im not t'go down t'pit today, but some'ow he didn't seem t'take no notice. Ah knowed it were going t'appen."

"You had a premonition then," interrupted Norman.

"Ah knowed," repeated the man.

Norman continued to ask questions about George Littlewood, to which the man in the room answered fully, going into great detail about George's early life.

Norman looked around from time to time as if wanting to sit down, but the man did not ask him to sit. So not wanting to be impolite to man in front of him, the whole interview was conducted standing in the corner of the room.

Eventually Norman decided he would have to go.

He put his pen and notebook away and said, "Well thanks, Mr Littlewood. It is Mr Littlewood isn't it?"

"Aye lad, Stanley Littlewood," came the reply.

"Well, I'll be off now," said Norman going to the door.

The man said nothing. Norman turned back as he reached for the door but the man had disappeared. He must have gone through the other door in the corner thought Norman.

He stepped out into the fresh air. I wonder if George was as strange as his brother Stanley, he thought.

Norman rushed back to the office eager to write his story. Everyone was out at lunch, but he decided he had to start his story.

"All right, Norman?"

Norman looked up at the editor.

"Yeah, yeah, Mr Bradley," he said impatiently. The telephone rang in the editor's office.

"That bloody phone! One day I'll have it disconnected," he cried striding out of the office.

Norman finished his story and carried the copy out to the editor's office. Bradley was still on the phone, so he put the story on his desk and went out.

Time for lunch he thought, feeling hungry. He bumped into Albert on the way out. I'll ask him later about Littlewood, he thought.

Refreshed after a ham sandwich and a couple of halves at the Swan, he returned to the office. Mr Bradley was talking with Albert and they looked up as he came in.

"This story, Norman, where did you get it?" asked the editor.

"Why?" asked Norman. "Are the facts wrong?"

"Well, no, I've checked with Albert – as you should have done – but who's this brother you mention?"

Norman told them and described the man even down to the missing fingers on his right hand. Albert turned grey and looked up at Bradley.

"What's the matter?" asked Norman.

Albert looked at him and said, "Well, as it happens, I know a bit about George Littlewood. But he didn't have a brother. He was an only child.

"But I used to know his father a bit. He sometimes came into my local pub. He used to be a miner too, but he died young from silicosis, you know with the dust. Well, his name was Stanley, but everyone in the pub knew him by his nickname – he got it after the accident in the pit," said Albert, his voice breaking up.

He paused.

"Well?" said Norman.

Albert stared at the wall for a moment and rather haltingly said, "His nickname was 'Three-fingered Stan'."

Granny Green

by Janet Griffiths

Granny Green fetched a jar from her kitchen and placed it down in front of them. She stood up on a chair and reached down her special book from the top shelf in her living room and blew off the dust from the top.

"Don't fret," she said to Petula Pink who was sitting in the corner with tears streaming down her face.

"This will sort it. I've never known it to fail."

She opened the pages of the old heavy black book until she found the one she wanted.

"Ah…I know what we need…honey, that's easy, brandy, I have that, a candle, I have plenty of those, but red rose petals, that's not so easy at this time of year, fresh ones that is, blue lavender is though, there's still a bush flowering late in the garden and I don't have a rose quartz crystal…hmmm."

Petula Pink wiped the tears from off her cheek, reached into her pocket and pulled out a large lump of pink crystal and placed it on the table in front of the jar.

"I know where there's a winter flowering rose bush" said Petula Pink. It's in my neighbour's garden."

"Can you go and fetch some petals then, my dear."

"I can try, but I'll have to be careful in case they see me."

"Off you go then, just be discreet and don't linger."

A short while later, the girl was back with a big smile on her face, red rose petals bursting out of her pockets.

"They almost saw me. I had to hide under a bush then sneak out because they were both looking out of the window."

"Good, let's add all the ingredients into the jar and light the candle, but first write your intention on this piece of paper and place it in the bottom."

They both watched in silence while the candle burnt down.

"It is done, now off you go, take the jar and throw it away at the crossroads. Then go home and wait...he will return."

The Last Reel

by Chris Freeman

"Joe!

"Joe!!

"Joseph!! Get up!"

Somewhere inside Joe's head a voice was pounding his sleeping brain. He didn't want to respond. He desperately wanted to go on dreaming and tried to get back to slumber, but the voice was ever louder and suddenly it burst onto his eardrums like a cascade of freezing water.

"Joe! It's interview day – get up!"

It was the voice of his mother, reminding him of yet another humiliation; the sort of humiliation that Joe had come to expect from interviews. He'd lost count of the interviewers that had turned him down almost as soon as he'd stepped through the doors of their offices. It would be different this time, his mother had told him, because the men at the water company were more sympathetic towards employing people like Joe, but Joe was still dreading the experience.

Joe was a creature of almost ritual habits; he got up at 7.45am and had a quick wash, got dressed and then straight down to a bowl of porridge laced with a big spoonful of honey and an even bigger dollop of yoghurt, which he always placed exactly in the centre of his favourite bowl.

Joe hated change and this morning he had to put on his best clothes for the interview, so he was already in a bad mood, but worse was the fact that he couldn't go to his 'Day Club' but had to get a bus in the opposite direction to go for this interview. An interview that he didn't want, for a job he would probably hate anyway and what was wrong with going to his special club every day anyway. He loved to play cards, or dominoes with his friends because he never lost. He always remembered where all of the cards were and after a few rounds he could always tell the players exactly what they had in their hands. Even when they all played darts, Joe was always picked to do the scoring because he could tell the players exactly what they needed as soon as the last dart hit the board. Good with numbers was Joe.

The bus driver made a quip about Joe going in the wrong direction and Joe explained that he was off to an interview today – at the water company. The driver bade him the very best of luck, but Joe could see he was just being polite.

There were three people in the interview room and Joe was introduced to them each in turn. There was the man who wanted a new worker, a man from HR, whatever that was, and a rather round lady who looked a bit like Joe's Mum and she made him feel comfortable. She was from Administration and would take notes. They all asked him lots of questions about himself and what he liked and disliked and what had he done before and Joe told them all about the club that he went to and how he loved to play cards and darts with his friends.

The main interviewer, the man who needed a new worker, asked Joe what his friends might think of him if he got the job at the sewage works. Joe wasn't sure about the details of the job, so he said he didn't know what his friends might think and anyway, he'd have more money than them, so he wouldn't mind what they all thought of him. Then the interviewer explained that the job was quite manual and involved working with sewage sludge. Joe would be kitted out in all the latest safety clothing in bright yellow and he would be given a huge squeegee so that when he went into the sewage sludge tank he could push all of the sludge to the end of the tank. As the sludge would be about six inches deep, it took quite a lot of effort to push it, and was Joe strong enough to do that all day? Joe flexed his muscles and said that he was very fit because they had a nice gym at the day club and he went with a helper three times a week. The interviewer laughed and said that Joe was just what they wanted for the job. He looked askance at his fellow interviewers and then at Joe.

"The actual title for this job is a Sewage Sludge Operative, but we call them 'The Shit Shoveller's Army' and it pays well," the man said. "All you need to do now is read through this application form and then sign it at the bottom."

Joe's heart almost thumped out of his chest and to the others in the room it must have looked as though Joe had been hit with a heart defibrillator; he jumped so. His head went down and he started to rock on his seat and his eyes began to fill with tears. The lady was quick to get to Joe's side to ask what the matter was and Joe sobbed that he couldn't read or write.

"Ah!" said the main man. "That could be a bit of a problem because you must be able to read the safety manuals and at the end of each day, you would have to complete a report on your day's work. I'm really sorry, but we can't employ you if you can't read and write."

As Joe was leaving the lady explained that he was entitled to his expenses for going to the interview and how much did he want? Joe was still reeling from the whole incident and was obviously distressed, so the lady pressed a £5 note into Joe's hand and said that she would sort out the paperwork later.

Outside, it was raining, not much, but the day seemed rather cool to poor old Joe, as set off for the bus station and as the slight breeze caught his face he shivered and felt suddenly very cold, so he headed into the first building close by. It was the George and Dragon Pub and it was warm inside. He had been into pubs before with his Mum, so he wasn't too fazed by the place.

The barman looked at Joe in a quizzical sort of way and then in an enquiring voice he asked Joe what he wanted. Joe looked at the man and said he just wanted to get warm please.

"You need a stiff whiskey!" said the barman.

Now, Joe knew he couldn't afford a drink because he never had any money except his bus fare. Then he felt the £5 note that was still crumpled up in his hand.

"Will this be enough?" he blurted, proffering the note.

It was obviously enough as the barman poured him a large whiskey and gave him £2 and a penny change.

Joe sat down and looked around him. There weren't may people in the pub as it was only late morning, but there was one older lady and a younger chap who were sat at a table close to Joe and the old lady nodded at him and smiled. Joe smiled back and quickly took a gulp from his glass of whiskey. He spluttered and almost spat out the whiskey, it burned so much, as he wasn't used to it.

The chap at the next table laughed out loud and then bellowed, "That caught you didn't it! You okay, mate?"

Poor old Joe could only smile at him and nod his head.

The elderly lady got up and Joe though she was going to come and sit with him, but she just walked past and as she did she touched his shoulder and explained that she was going to play the fruit machine, so wish her luck. Joe almost jumped up at her.

"Can I watch, can I watch, can I watch?" Joe repeatedly asked.

The lady looked closely at Joe's face and began to realise that he was somehow different, although she couldn't work out why. The way he jumped up and repeated his request was odd, but she said she didn't mind him watching.

"But don't press any of the buttons!" she told him.

The fruit machine gobbled pound after pound of the old lady's money without dropping so much as a penny and then just as she was about to hold the first reel which was showing a melon, Joe caught her hand and just said "NO!" in such a loud voice it made her jump.

"Don't hold it." Joe said. "If you let the thing go on, in four more goes all the melons will be together." She looked at him – deeply into his eyes.

She then realised that he was deadly serious.

Okay, she thought, *There's something odd about this guy and maybe he's got something I don't know about.*

She humoured him and pushed her last pound into the machine. She spun the thing three times and then realised she was out of credit and was one spin short. She looked at Joe, as if for support.

"I got a pound," said Joe eagerly, and before she knew it, he'd shoved it into the machine and pressed the 'Go' button. Click – one melon. Click - two melons. Click – three melons. Clunk, clunk, whirr, whirr, and pound coins came tumbling out like rain on a summer's day; all fifty of them. The old lady's son rushed over to see what had happened.

"He's only gone and robbed the machine," the old lady said.

Joe was jumping and clapping his hands.

"Next one! Next one! Next one! Play the next one!"

Joe's excitement was catching, and they moved to the second machine on the other side of the bar.

The old lady looked at Joe.

"This is your baby," she said. "It was your pound what dropped all that cash, not mine."

Joe fed the machine and pressed the 'Go' button and just kept shoving the coins in and pressing the button, without so much as holding any of the reels, even when they had two of something in a row. After ten minutes about £20 had been put into the machine and Joe looked at the reels as they spun round. Then he did a strange thing and for no apparent reason he held two of the reels for two goes. He then released those and held one of them for another go. He looked at the old lady and her son and a big grin came over his face. He nodded towards the machine and put another coin into the slot. He pressed the button and away the machine whirred yet again with nothing happening and then the next go was the same. Before starting the machine again, Joe rubbed his hands together in a Scrooge like way and smiled at the other two. He pressed the button for the machine to start. Click – one melon. Click - two melons. Click – three melons. Clunk, clunk, whirr, whirr, and the pound coins came tumbling out again; all fifty of them.

"Oi you! That's my 'oliday money your takin' there!" yelled the barman.

The old lady looked across at him and just said, "Beginner's luck mate. Just beginner's luck."

"Oh, I'm not lucky," said Joe, I just lost an interview for a job at the sewage works."

He then went on to tell the old lady and her son about his experience at the interview. The old lady sympathised with Joe and said that she was called Dot and her son was Jim and they both understood his predicament. Jim had been a bouncer at the doors of nightclubs, but one day he bounced someone too hard and he was put in prison for a month. Now nobody would employ him, so he was on the dole. She herself had been retired early because of cuts at her firm, so they were both a bit strapped for cash, but she played the machines just hoping for a lucky win.

Dot quizzed Joe about how he knew that the machines would do what he wanted them to, and he said that it was easy because he knew what was coming next. Dot and Jim looked at each other and then back at Joe.

"How do you know what's coming next?" Dot asked and Joe just replied that he knew all the ways that the reels worked.

"You mean you know what's coming 'cos you remember all the sequences?" asked Jim.

Joe looked puzzled and said he didn't know what that word meant, but he knew all the ways that the melons and lemons and things could stop and he just altered them to suit how he wanted the three in a row. It was easy, but he had to let the machine show him all the ways it could stop first.

Dot took Joe's arm and looked at Jim.

"NEXT PUB!" she commanded.

Well, Joe repeated the whole exercise in the next pub, much to the non-amusement of the landlord. They beat a hasty retreat and quickly moved to another pub, where they found a machine that had four reels and paid out £100. There was a man playing the machine and Joe eagerly looked over his shoulder. He stopped and glared at Joe as if to warn him off. Dot stepped up and whispered something in the chap's ear. The glare turned to a smile and he went back to playing, but it wasn't long before he quit and that was Joe's chance to step in. He put five £1 coins into the machine and held one reel, but let the others spin for several goes before releasing the first reel. Continuing to play he only stopped reels occasionally and very soon he was rubbing his hands again and he turned to give Dot a big smile. Jim sat patiently at a nearby table, watching the proceedings in case anything went wrong.

Joe spun the reels. Click – one melon. Click - two melons. Click – three melons. Click – four melons. Clunk, clunk, whirr, whirr, and one hundred pound coins came tumbling out and spilled all over the pub carpet. They quickly gathered up the coins, beat a hasty retreat and went into a little café down the road to count their winnings. Joe was adamant that they split the take three ways because that was what best of friends did.

They then agreed to meet up the next day at the bus station at 9 o'clock.

As Joe headed for the bus home he thought how the day was suddenly much brighter, as he realised that he really did have two new friends and he went home on the bus a happy man. Slightly tipsy, but happy.

At home, Joe slipped past his mum with a complaint that he didn't get the job because he couldn't read and write and went straight up to his room. All of the money went under his mattress. His mum thought nothing of the swift entrance and disappearing act to his bedroom. After all, she had seen the same thing many times before and she was just a little sad for him.

The next day, at exactly 9am, Joe met up with Dot and Jim at the bus station and they went off around as many of the pubs in town as they could get to in a day, cleaning out every fruit machine as they went. They actually managed to visit eight pubs that day, with a total of seventeen machines, which netted what seemed like a small fortune to Joe. Once again they went to the café to split the take and when Joe got home, the same thing; the money went under the mattress.

Joe's head was spinning like the fruit machines. He'd never had so much fun and never really been so pleased to be able to use his amazing skill. Playing cards and dominoes at the club and remembering who had what was never as much fun as all that money pouring out of the fruit machines, having remembered all of the reels. And what was that new word that Jim had taught him – see – kwence. Yes, that was it – see-kwence.

Being a creature of habit Joe had insisted that the trio continue their work on the rest of the pubs in town, but Dot had bigger ideas. They met at the bus station as agreed, but this time they headed for a different bus. Dot said that the destination was a secret, like a mystery tour, but Joe didn't like that and Jim could see that he was a bit distressed.

"BLACKPOOL! That's where we're going to. You'll see, there's thousands of fruit machines."

Jim put his arm around Joe's shoulders and gave him a great big man-hug. As he did so, he noticed two unlikely looking gents in dark suits and being an ex-bouncer and used to odd characters, Jim was a bit suspicious and even more so when they got onto the same bus to go to Blackpool.

Joe was still a bit nervous, so Dot and Jim explained all about Blackpool and the seaside and how there were thousands of fruit machines. More than you could ever think of. Well, Joe's eyes lit up at the thought and suddenly he was looking forward to the day out.

They arrived at Blackpool and as they got out of the station, Joe was like a child with a bucket and spade who just can't wait to get to the beach. Dot pointed the way to the seafront and Joe was off, like a bat out of hell, with Dot and Jim firmly attached to a hand each.

At the first arcade, needless to say, Joe did his stuff on every machine he played and before lunch they had netted another small fortune; less the money that they had to put into the machines, so that Joe could remember all of the sequences. They ended up with so much money that Dot had to go into the nearest branch of her bank and convert most the pound coins into notes. Whilst Dot was in the bank, Jim and Joe waited outside in the warm spring sunshine and Jim noticed the two suspicious looking suited gents that he'd seen before. When Dot came out he whispered to her that he was bit suspicious of them. Were they following them?

Dot, being the artful one, hatched a plan. They acted quite normally and went into a pub that sold food to get their lunch. Whilst eating Dot noticed the two suited gents at the other end of the bar. When they had all finished eating she told Jim to leave on his own and head for the train station and she and Joe would catch up in about fifteen minutes. Sure enough, one of the gents followed Jim and Dot waited until they were well gone before she told Joe she was just going to the toilet before they left. Out of sight, in the toilet, Dot phoned Jim on his mobile and told him to get a taxi from the station and come back and pick them up at the pub. They were thus all quickly reunited and on their way to Poulton-Le-Fylde railway station. To be sure of not being followed, and to cover their tracks, they feigned going into the station for a train only to re-emerge seconds later to get another taxi back to Blackpool to start on a good afternoon's work raiding the fruit machines, free of any tail.

Of course, it goes without saying that Joe managed to empty every machine that he played.

By now, Joe's bed was beginning to heave under the weight of bank notes, so when his Mum was out one day Joe took up some of the floorboards in his room and stuffed the money between the joists.

After their day out at Blackpool they went to Skegness for the day and then to just about every place between that had anything like a decent number of fruit machines worth raiding.

Once or twice Dot was sure that they had somebody following them, but she was always up to the challenge and always managed to dodge the tail before carrying on with the task in hand, raiding fruit machines!

Jim was soon able to buy himself a little car and they went farther and farther afield to raid the fruit machines. Dot was always careful not to take them to too many pubs or arcades in one area before moving on and in that way they never attracted any attention to what they were doing. For well over two years they carried on, every day a new location and every day Joe returned home with his booty, all to be stuffed under the floorboards.

All good things must come to an end though and it came in a most surprising way. Joe had always had a mobile phone for emergencies, but he had never used it and often forgot to charge it, but this morning, quite early, it rang whilst he was still at home. It was Dot, telling him to move all of his money in a hurry. The call cut off abruptly and Joe began to panic. He didn't like this, and he started to sweat and rocked on his bed wondering just what he could do. His Mum had heard his phone ringing and went upstairs to investigate, but before she had got to Joe's room, the front doorbell had rung and she hurried back down the stairs.

The uniformed and plain-clothes police officers at the door produced some papers and a very shocked Mum let them in. She called Joe down and it was then that one of the officers said that they were arresting Joe on suspicion of money laundering, and the officer read Joe his rights. He asked Joe if he understood what he had just said and Joe sort of nodded, but didn't speak. That was enough for the officer to handcuff Joe and lead him away. As Joe was being led away, two more officers appeared with a sniffer-dog. The officers took the dog upstairs and began to search Joe's room. In just a few moments, the dog had located Joe's money haul, so they started gathering up all of the notes from under the bed and the floorboards. Although they had several very large plastic sacks to accommodate the cash, they still had to go out to their car for more bags; such was the volume of money.

The lawyer that Joe's Mum had found, out of the Yellow Pages, was very sympathetic to Joe. He listened intently to all of Joe's explanations and how he had worked with Dot and Jim. Dot was the brains to make sure that they weren't found out and Jim was the bodyguard to make sure that they were always safe with their money; two really good friends. The lawyer sat back and laughed heartily when Joe had finished and called the senior police officer back to the interview room. The two of them spoke quietly for a while and then they went over to Joe, who was sitting, rocking in a corner, with his Mum at his side. The lawyer asked Joe if he would mind doing a test for them and Joe said he was okay with that, so the lawyer wrote down a whole column of numbers and showed them to Joe. As quickly as he showed the numbers he took them away again. He then proceeded to ask Joe what the tenth number was and the second and so on. Of course, Joe got every one correct. He then asked Joe to tell them what the numbers of all the buses at the local bus station were and where each of the buses stopped. The seventh stop for the number twenty-seven: "Jacob Street!" and so on. For ages they went on. The police officer just sat there, amazed at Joe's ability to remember every stop, of every bus, running from the bus station. Every sequence of numbers they tried, Joe correctly identified the numbers. Joe told them that he could remember every sequence of every reel on the fruit machines, even if they had five or six reels, but the trick was always to remember the sequence of the last reel.

"We thought that you were laundering money for the other two," said the policeman. "It was the tax office that put us onto you when your mate Jim stopped going to sign on for the dole and then bought himself a new car; and you haven't got a traceable bank account. You even dodged all of the people we sent to follow you, so we naturally though that you were up to no good."

He then asked Joe how he had met up with Dot and Jim and Joe explained that he met them in a pub after his failed interview at the water company because he couldn't read and write.

"Well, you don't need a regular job now because we've counted most of that money and there's over a million pounds in hard cash."

"My goodness!" exclaimed the lawyer. "You're a genius, a millionaire and you can't even read and write! Just think what you could have achieved if you could read and write. What would you have been if you could have done?"

"I would have been a shit shoveler at the sewage works," said Joe.

Tales from Happy Valley

From a true story.

Savant syndrome is a rare condition in which people with developmental disorders have one or more areas of expertise, ability, or brilliance that are in contrast to their overall limitations. Some people who have savant syndrome are autistic, but some are not. Not all autistic people have savant syndrome and not all people with savant syndrome have autistic disorder.

Joe is a savant and is one very special person. A little of his story is told here. I had the privilege of meeting Joe in The Peat Pitts Pub, Ogden, West Yorkshire, where he was banned from playing the fruit machine. The pub is now called The Moorlands.

What If?

by Janet Griffiths

What if you woke up one morning and found yourself in the twenty-year old version of yourself again? You look down at your hands, gone is the wrinkly skin, the age spots and the lines. You take a stretch and your body feels so good, so alive; gone is the mild aching and creakiness you usually feel when you wake up. You bound out of bed, full of life and vitality and take a look in the mirror. Your eyes are large and clear; gone are the bags you normally see under them, the crows feet, the frown lines in the centre of your forehead. Your face looks glowing and youthful, it looks so good.

You rub your hands over your body; it feels strong and taut and the skin is so smooth, plumped up and dewy. You feel amazing and little bubbles of joy rise up from your heart as you smile to yourself.

You look at your clothes, but find it hard to find any that will fit your newly renewed body. You sift through the neatly folded tops in your chest of drawers and flick through the trousers in your wardrobe, but they are huge…and very frumpy.

Then you remember, at the back of the wardrobe is a bag of clothes you've kept for years, just for sentimental reasons, not seriously thinking you'd ever wear them again.

You empty the bag of clothes on to your bed and pull out a pair of jeans and a jumper. You vaguely remember wearing them; they are so 80s, but they fit and look pretty good!

You bound downstairs into the kitchen, you have so much energy it's literally pouring out of you. Standing with his back to you in an old scruffy dressing gown and slippers is your husband. He looks so old; you've never noticed before how old he actually looks. He's making two cups of tea...his usual morning routine.

"Morning, love," he says as usual.

"Morning, dear," you reply.

He turns round with the tea in his hand, his jaw drops open and he is transfixed, mesmerised by this new version of yourself. His face visibly drains of colour and his hands start shaking. The tea slops about and spills over the sides of the mug.

You reach out to help him, you take the tea and place it down on the kitchen worktop.

He is rooted to the spot, his eyes wider than you've ever seen them before. He looks as though he wants to speak but no sound will come out of his mouth.

You drink the tea quickly, grab your coat and bag and float outside waving goodbye.

"I think shopping is in order today," you say. "See you later darling."

As you look back your husband has slumped into a chair, spilling his cup of tea all over his dressing gown and pyjamas.

— ❧ ❧ —

The Baptism

by Alison Milner

I prod her, Peat Bog Peg. My fingers hesitant, afraid of what I might awake. She's surprisingly hard and rigid for a knitted doll. The same dirty-pink colour as the jumper Grandma knitted for me when I was a child. It had chaffed my skin. The doll's skin is coarse and prickly. She must have been made from identical wool.

Grandma said Peg was a Grindylow. A water spirit who lives in the peat pools, which gape open-mouthed with acidic lips; ragged holes in a fustian textile of moorland.

Grandma made Peat Bog Peg speak, contorting the stitched lips so that they appeared puckered, just like her own mouth. Terrifying, exciting tales about people drowned in murky depths.

I put Peat Bog Peg in my pocket. I can't just throw her away. I'll take her for a walk and rewild her in natural habitat.

Moorland stretches around me like the clenched fist of a mottled hand. Knuckle ridges scarred with ancient causeways.

The wind flings words, berates the isolated stone buildings crouched in hillside clefts. The sky is ashen with streaks of iridescent light, like searchlights from hovering spacecraft.

White bones of dried gorse and heather snap gunfire beneath my boots. The tufted grass feels like coarse human hair. Blonde with highlights of ginger. Thick clumps have blown onto a barbed-wire fence, where it waves as the manes of mythological lions.

The stone seeps words, they are hewn from rock, carved by millstone grit; particles of the dead. Spongy terrain dictates my tilting gait as I balance precariously on a revolving earth. My face is raw. My mouth tastes acrid.

A Green Man appears, blurred on a water-colour horizon. My vision focuses and he becomes a hiker.

I remember heather cures coughs and anxiety. I remove Peat Bog Peg respectfully from my jacket and baptise her Eve. I carry her home to bring me good fortune.

The Smile

by Joan Watson

The gaslights popped in the shadowy classroom as I frantically tied up small parcels of crepe paper, each one containing a chocolate wrapped in silver foil. The end of my first Christmas term as a teacher and I was so tired I could hardly twist the ends to transform them into crackers. Only four more to go. The bell rang and my class of forty-nine children started to pile out of the door, excitedly grabbing crackers before pushing their way down the paper chain bedecked corridor, their excited voices slowly fading.

Hanging back, Patricia decided that now was the time to discuss an important theological question, leaning against my arm she sleepily asked,

"Miss, what will Baby Jesus get for Christmas? Will he get a chocolate sweet?"

I shook my head and answered without thinking,

"No, Patricia, Baby Jesus won't get any presents on Christmas Day; his will come when the three kings bring them after Christmas."

I put a cracker into the hands of a small boy who took it, quickly disappearing out of the classroom door.

"Remember, Ronnie, don't eat it now. Keep it to hang on your Christmas tree."

I shouted after him, knowing full well that he would have the paper off before he reached the cloakroom.

Returning to the business of making up the next crepe paper parcel the three remaining little girls gathered round me in a circle. They had all been absent yesterday and foolishly I had not bothered to make them a cracker the night before, thinking they wouldn't return before the end of term. But in a school where the children would not find very much on Christmas morning the few small things given to them on the last day of term were important.

Looking up at Paula in a red tartan kilt and green jumper, fair hair encircling her head, I thought back to the first day of term. Pushed through the classroom door by an older sister I found her a seat, but when asked her name she couldn't reply she was so frightened. Filthy matted hair surrounded a small, dirt-ingrained face and her soiled dress hung off her, faded and torn.

By ten o'clock her smell had become so noticeable to the other children, as well as myself, that Mrs McGuire the school helper was sent for. Taking Paula by the hand they headed for the bathroom and after a stand up bath, hair wash and clean clothes from the school supplies the little girl returned smiling and happy in a pink party frock.

The next day she returned in her rags, grubby as ever. Her mother had sold the pink dress. Mrs McGuire persevered for the rest of the week unsuccessfully, so on the following Monday at home time, Paula's school clothes were taken off and her own put back on. This became Mrs McGuire's first job of the day, to wash and dress Paula. Tonight the last day of term she had intentionally forgotten to change Paula.

"All done now!" I said five minutes later as I handed the last cracker to Elisabeth.

"Go straight home now; it's getting quite dark. Happy Christmas."

"Happy Christmas, Miss," they all shouted as they ran out of the classroom.

Their elated voices echoed down the stairs, through the cloakroom and out into the yard until the back door slammed shut.

I stood in the rare silence gazing at my stripped classroom, the small Christmas Tree standing forlornly in a corner, the walls cleared of paintings. Small iron desks stood in neat rows, each with their seats up while the smell of stale milk and chalk dust lingered heavily in the air. I was too tired to do anything else here, the thought of home with its warm fire was enticing. Finding one last chocolate to eat on the bus home, I swept the muddle from the top of my desk into a bag, grabbed my coat and scarf from the cupboard and heaving a sigh of relief, left the classroom. It was the end of an interminably long term with many mistakes made along the way, but now a sense of elation left me lightheaded and a bit dizzy.

Most of the staff had gone by now, probably on the bus I had just missed. Waving cheerily to the Caretaker, I stepped out of the school gate, hurrying across the road to the bus stop. The sky, now black and overcast, combined with an icy wind to send tiny snowflakes swirling around my feet. The senior and junior schools were all out now and groups of children ran along the pavement trying to find enough snow to make a snowball. With fifteen minutes to wait until the next bus came

St Joseph's Church towered over me, its grey roof just visible against the blackening sky.

The church door was half open and with my scarf whipping round my face I decided a quick prayer and some respite from the cold would be a good idea.

In the gathering dusk the church was in semi darkness with only a murky light radiating from the candles in front of several statues of saints and the red sanctuary lamp hanging above the altar. There was a welcoming aroma of incense, dust and candle grease. Above the sound of the wind moaning through the open door I could hear the sound of children singing.

Peering through the gloom I could see children in front of the large stable beside the altar and recognised them at once. Elisabeth in her brown coat, which was far too long - a hand me down from one of her five sisters. Paula, half her size, in a skimpy jacket, long hair hanging over her shoulders and Patricia with her red woollen hat slipping off the back of her head as usual.

What were they doing? I had told them to go straight home. As they finished singing what sounded like "Away in a Manger" I crept out into the porch and waited, looking along the road for my bus and was just in time to see Sister Monica quietly coming out of the side door of the church looking very furtive. The children came down the aisle, half running, half walking and as they came into the porch they saw me and ran towards me.

"Miss, Miss, I gave Baby Jesus a present of my chocolate, and guess what?" cried Patricia, "Mary said, 'Thank you.'"

"No," I said in mock amazement.

"Yes, and then I gave her mine and she said, 'Thank you,'" said Elisabeth.

Paula stood, bright eyes shining, cheeks rosy red. "And...," she whispered, "Baby Jesus smiled at me."

Out of the corner of my eye I could see Sister Monica being blown along towards us, her head dress flapping like the wings of a giant bird, black skirts blowing like sails in the wind.

"Children, shouldn't you be home by now?" she said, smiling. "It's starting to snow."

The flakes were larger now and the snow thick on the ground.

"Sister Monica! We gave baby Jesus our chocolates," said Elisabeth excitedly, "and Mary said, 'Thank you.'"

"And we sang him 'Away in a Manger'," joined in Patricia.

"And baby Jesus smiled," whispered Paula.

"What kind children! I've got a present for you," she said, and from the depths of her black skirts she produced three bars of chocolate. "Happy Christmas, now straight home."

The three girls chattering with excitement ran down the lane beside the church and I watched them disappear into the darkness. I turned and saw Sister Monica wave as she crossed the road and entered the brightly lit convent.

Turning up my collar and peering along the road, I searched in vain for the welcoming glow of bus headlights approaching. Seeing nothing but blackness through the swirling snow, I had just enough time for a quick visit to the crib. Walking down the aisle, candlelight flickered and danced on the walls of the wooden stable, as my footsteps echoed harshly in the empty church. Joseph stood protectively looking down at Mary and the small baby lying in the manger. A woollen lamb, rather the worse for wear after years of being patted, lay in front of them while an ox and a donkey stood guard and a shepherd knelt in worship alongside them.

It was very peaceful, with even the noise of traffic being muffled by the snow. I knelt down to pray and, looking round to check I was alone, impulsively took the last chocolate out of my pocket and placed it in the manger, whispering, "Here's a present for you baby Jesus."

Turning round to go back down the aisle a small voice clearly said, "Thank you" and to this day, I could swear I saw baby Jesus smile.

What Is Behind the Curtain?

by Janet Griffiths

The huge red curtain stretches across the stage. The lights have dimmed, and the audience is hushed in expectation, only a quiet rustle from bags of sweets and popcorn and the sound of quiet breathing. Expectation.

We are waiting. Waiting for the show to begin. But it's not beginning, nothing's happening.

Time passes. The rustling gets louder and the breathing more impatient. The audience look at each other, to the left, to the right, behind and in front at the curtain.

There is a gentle movement from behind it. Nothing major, just a gentle rustle. Is something happening? Is something about to happen? It certainly should be by now.

The curtain stops rustling and is still again. The sounds of eating and crunching get louder and a low murmuring starts.

People murmur to the left, to the right, behind. The audience is polite, waiting in polite expectation. But still nothing happens, the curtain is still.

Stamp, stamp, someone is stamping their feet. Others join in. The stamping gets louder and more forceful. More and more people join in. The whole audience is stamping and now clapping. The stamping and clapping gets louder and louder until it's deafening.

But there's still no action from behind the curtain.

It starts to ripple. It starts at one corner and moves slowly, rippling along the whole length.

The whole curtain is rippling and moving. The whole audience is stamping and clapping.

Maybe this is what's supposed to happen. Maybe the curtain won't open and we'll never find out what's behind it. Maybe we're just here for the experience.

But if this is what we've paid for, we've paid a lot of money just to sit in an auditorium with a rippling curtain in front of us.

I try not to feel frustrated but I am. This is not what I expected. I look to the left, to the right and behind me.

The house lights go down as my darkened soul leaves my body.

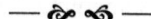

The Last Acorn

by Chris Freeman

Pete's mobile phone buzzed and vibrated incessantly in his pocket and it made him jump. It always did, but at least he didn't miss any calls because of too much noise. His old mobile was well overdue for recycling. It wasn't fancy, not even any good for taking pictures, and its ring was so pathetic that if there was any noise around he couldn't hear it, so it vibrated and buzzed instead. He looked briefly at the caller display and noted it was his brother – Big Bruv he called him, for he was all of twenty-two stone and six feet five.

"Hi there, Big Bruv – what goes?"

"It's going to be fine and sunny this weekend; fancy camping?" Pete was asked.

"Don't mind if we do. We haven't seen each other for ages. Where at, Headnut Woods?" said Pete.

"Where else?" questioned Big Bruv. "And I'll beat you with the catapult too. Don't forget to bring yours and collect plenty of acorns from the old oak at the wayside because there aren't any at the campsite."

Pete's reply was quite terse.

"Listen, if we're goin' Friday, don't you be late; I know you. An hour extra at the lab and then you'll blame the traffic."

"Just you have the kettle on, that's all. An' don't forget the acorns!" bellowed Big Bruv.

Pete returned the phone to his pocket and forgot about it.

Pete didn't forget to collect a load of acorns though, but only enough for himself. He knew that his brother would collect a load as well, just to make sure that they had a good contest. The old oak stood about a mile from the edge of the woods and it was another mile to the campsite, so gathering enough acorns before getting to the site was essential. Pete stuffed about twenty acorns into his jacket pocket and made off to the camp site. The catapult thing was all in fun really and they enjoyed the banter that went with it. They usually picked an empty baked bean can and set it up about twenty yards away and then took turns at taking pot-shots until one of them hit it. The other would then have to fill the can with beer and drink it in one go. This was always guaranteed to get them both more than a bit tipsy within an hour or so, but it got harder and harder to hit the can anyway, so in the end they would give up and start chatting. Putting-the-world-to-rights as they say and when it got dark, they'd sleep till morning.

Pete carefully placed the blade of the hand axe on top of the kindling wood and tapped it on the old tree stump. He always marvelled at how the blade bit into the wood and held it, as if in a steely grip. He lifted both axe and wood, and with one smart tap, he cleaved the wood in two. He picked up one piece, the larger of the two, and deftly repeated the exercise. This was something he was good at, having practised for something like twenty years. Pete couldn't remember when he and his brother first started coming to the woods, and his brain couldn't start thinking about mathematical calculations whilst he was chopping wood. He'd tried that before and failed, nearly cutting off the end of his finger. No, concentration was the name of the game. When he cleaved the kindling wood, he prided himself in never actually dropping the hand axe far enough to sink it into the old tree stump. There was a practised art in just giving the axe enough impetus to split the wood, but not hit the stump.

Big Bruv had been right about the weather, thought Pete, *It's a really beautiful summer evening and so quiet, I bet that if anyone heard me chopping this wood now, they'd think I was a woodpecker.*

Pete picked up another piece of kindling, getting quite lost in this simple, repetitive chore. Tapping the blade down once more he then picked up the axe, with the kindling wood attached to it and made to deftly cleave this next piece, but the silence was pierced by the most blood-curdling scream. Such was the shock to Pete's system that the axe fell with a mighty thud and stuck firmly into the end grain of the old rotten tree trunk. Suddenly, his senses were hyper-acute and he could hear voices, but as to there whereabouts he couldn't tell. The woods were supposed to be haunted, but in all the time they'd been going there, they'd never seen or heard a thing. It was just another one of those urban myths put about by the landowners to keep people out.

Suddenly, out of the trees and into the clearing burst a group of figures. Pete looked at them horrified and counted five as they all emerged into view. Pete made a grab for the hand axe, but it was stuck fast in the stump.

Mid-twenties, he thought, *and trouble written all over them.*

"'Allo, 'allo. Wot we got 'ere then?" said the tall yob out in front.

Pete stayed silent.

"Wha's a marrer – cat got ya tongue?" taunted the yob. "Or maybe yu'd like me to cut it out for ya!" he cackled and brandished an enormous carving knife in Pete's direction.

"Yer – cut 'is tongue out," demanded one of the others in the group.

Then, almost as one voice, they chanted, "Yeah, cut it out, cut it out! Cut 'is tongue out!"

Pete's blood ran cold.

Where the hell was Big Bruv when he was needed, he was already an hour late, thought Pete, *and I need the cavalry now!*

The lead yob advanced menacingly, wielding the knife above his head like a silver flag.

"Come on then – get your loverly knife here then!" he taunted again.

Pete heard the high-pitched, whistling whine, and instinctively knew what it was. In a split second he knew what it was, but how? Where from?

The acorn whistled past Pete's ear with only millimetres to spare and he flinched instinctively to one side. He felt the draft, but watched spellbound as the acorn struck the knife-wielding yob right between the eyes. It stopped him dead in his tracks. Half a second later, a second acorn whizzed past Pete's ear. Once again, the yob was hit, this time in his ear. The first acorn stunned him, but this one made him cry out in pain. The next two hit his head and made him drop to his knees in pain.

Quick shooting, Bruv, thought Pete, *and damned accurate, too! Well done!*

The second yob fared no better, nor any of the others as a tirade of acorns whistled and whizzed past Pete to hit them repeatedly about their heads. By now the first yob was on his feet and there was a distinctly glazed look on his face and he was ashen white. He looked past Pete and pointed.

"How?" he stammered, "How d... d... d... d... did you...?"

But he was already turning on his heels.

"RUN!!" he screamed, "RUN!!"

The others took his lead and fled. The last one to exit the clearing looked back, but just as he left, he tripped and fell. As he stood up, Pete could see that he, too, was as white as a sheet.

Pete's heart took a mighty leap and he physically jumped as his phone vibrated and buzzed in his pocket.

What the..., he thought and yanked the offending mobile out.

"YES!" he blurted, "WHAT?"

"Oh touchy – touchy" remonstrated the familiar voice of Big Bruv. "What's eaten your goat then?"

"Where the hell are you?" Pete demanded.

And then, in a quiet, calm, and rather sarcastic voice, his brother replied, "Well, if you must know, I really did get held up, but not at the office. There's been a nasty accident on the main road, not far from the woods, and someone's got knocked over. In fact, according to the lady about ten cars in front of me, there were about four or five guys all ran out into the road and got hit by a truck about an hour ago. We've only just been allowed through now they've all been carted off by ambulance. I should be with you in about twenty minutes. Have you got the kettle on yet?"

"Sorry about that," said Pete, after a moment's stunned silence, "been a bit odd here: I'll explain when you get here. I just need a bit more firewood and I'll have a cuppa ready on arrival. See you soon, bye."

Pete dropped the phone back into his trouser pocket and suddenly felt chill. He put his hands into his jacket pockets for a warm and almost jumped out of his skin again. His left hand, which should have found a whole load of acorns, didn't. He fumbled into the corners and came up with just two acorns. He pulled one out and looked at it amazed for few seconds. The two acorns were alone, bereft, with no others to swell his pocket, but how? Thoughts raced through his brain and then the truth suddenly hit home. He hadn't felt the acorns being taken from his pocket, but gone they certainly had and mighty quickly too. The chill came back and he shivered. He spun around as if to look for someone, but he knew he was alone, so that was daft really, but he did it anyway.

I know what I'll do, he thought.

He rummaged in his back-pack to find his own catapult and when he did, he popped one of the acorns into the soft leather pouch. Half drawing the strong elastic back he looked around for a target and found, about twenty yards away, the offensive carving knife that had been dropped earlier by the yob.

Yes, he said to himself, I feel lucky tonight, and drew back the elastic.

He took careful aim and let fly. He heard the familiar whizzing, whistling sound as the acorn sped to its target and he watched, almost as if it was all in slow motion, as the acorn struck the very edge of the knife's blade and split cleanly into two pieces. A shiver went down his spine and he reached into his pocket for his phone.

He dialled the last caller. "Hello, Bruv, can you do me a favour and bring some more acorns from the big oak?"

"You been practising, have you?" asked his brother.

"Well, not exactly," said Pete, "but I'm down to my last acorn. See you soon. Bye!"

Pete managed to free the axe and, having cut enough wood, he lit the fire and put the billy-can over it to brew the tea. He idly picked up the newspaper that he'd used to light the fire and flicked its remaining pages to see if there was anything worth reading. Finding the cryptic crossword he tried the first clue that took his eye. 6 across: 7 letters. Headnut Woods – don't go there (anagram).

Never was any good at damn crosswords, he thought to himself and threw the paper on the fire.

He fumbled in his left pocket, took out his last acorn and carefully placed it into the leather pouch of his trusty catapult. He walked to the other side of the clearing and once again he took careful aim and let fly. This time the acorn was ghostly silent as it sped to its target. No whistle, no buzz, just a clean flight path straight to the heart of the fire. As it struck home it sent a great, blinding shower of sparks skywards and then it burned so brightly that he could feel the heat twenty yards away.

Tales from Happy Valley

The billy-can instantly boiled and whistled its heart out! The last acorn had done its stuff.

The Stunt

by Janet Griffiths

"Hi Lauren, it's Danny."

"Danny, good to hear from you."

My phone hasn't rung for days, in fact my life has become very dull and meaningless. Endless workouts, acrobatic practices (pretty difficult in my little flat), a couple of casual shifts in Morrisons and binge-watching Netflix.

"Lauren, I've got a job for you."

"A job!" My heart starts to quicken, I can feel it thud, thud, thudding in my chest the way it always does when I get an assignment.

"You're good with acrobatics, aren't you?"

"Acrobatics, am I? Mmmm," I mutter, my mind racing, "What's the job?"

"We're sending you to a little town in West Yorkshire. They need a double for the main character. Tomorrow and Friday, two days filming, good money!"

"I'll take it," I say trying not to get too excited.

Better than packing groceries in Morrisons!

"Okay, I'm emailing you the brief now. Get back in touch if you have any queries."

I put the phone down, stare into the receiver and turn on my laptop. 'Eco-films': the film company that cares about the environment. In production now, an action-adventure movie for the planet.

I arrive at the base at precisely 7 a.m. the next morning and am greeted by a pretty, youngish woman, looking efficient with a clipboard in her hand.

"I'll take you to see James to explain what's going on."

James is sitting inside one of a group of caravans surrounded by five grungy-looking guys, obviously the crew. James is also rather grungy-looking, dreads piled up under a large cap that looks like it's made from hessian and wearing a large holey jumper that's seen better days. I assume he's the Director.

They turn round to face me and look me up and down. No-one speaks.

"Hi," I say cheerily, smiling my best eyes and teeth smile.

"You don't look much like an Eco-Warrior," James mutters.

Eco-Warrior! I had no idea I was to be an Eco-Warrior; I have no idea what an Eco-Warrior does or even looks like! My smile freezes on my face, and I try hard not to look uncomfortable. Damn it. Danny, you never fill me in properly!

"Okay, I'll explain. Hair and Makeup can give you a makeover, the scenes we're shooting today and tomorrow are up on the moors and down by the river. Today, you're head of a group who are chasing a bunch of posh nobs who are burning the peat and heather on the moors. So, it's a frantic chase with some acrobatics thrown in: front flips, back flips, dives etc. See you on set in an hour."

Why would a group of 'posh nobs' be burning peat and heather on the moors? And who are these 'posh nobs'? I take his word for it and step out to find the Hair and Makeup van.

Well, that's the strangest 'makeover' I've ever had. My usual long glossy locks are now matted together with what appears to be mud. I swear they've used real mud, certainly smells like it, my hair is twisted into a grimy mess of dreadlocks which are now hanging heavily down my back and all my makeup's been removed. Horrors! I'm dressed in an old oilskin jacket that's about two sizes too big for me, combat trousers and a pair of army boots that are pinching my toes. Damn Danny again, he can't even get my sizes right! I can't recognise myself, anyway. Eco-Warriors here I come!

The moors are vast, stretching for miles in each direction. Although it's pretty windy, the sun's out and it's a bright clear day. I'm sitting in the back of a Range Rover with my double, Stacey, the star. James is fussing around outside, positioning his crew for the shoot. A group of support actors mill around, looking bored already. I've checked my emails, Facebook and Instagram and am now scrolling Twitter, looking for something interesting to read. Stacey stares nonchalantly out of the window, obviously not a great conversationalist. Why do I always forget about the tediousness of these jobs and not come prepared? But then I remember Morrisons!

After what seems like an age, but probably isn't, we are called. Action at last!

James explains the shot we're going to do. Stacey, the real Eco-Warrior, is going to scream and yell. At this point I am to charge over the moors with my trusty fellow Eco-Warriors behind me. He wants me to do a front-flip at the end of the charge. The 1st Assistant Director will flap his arms in the air when he wants me to perform.

We're going for a take.

"Rolling…and…action."

Stacey yells and screams, and we take off. I feel like Queen Boadicea leading an uprising, bits of mud falling off my dreads which are flailing around my head. Bet Queen Boadicea didn't have to wear a pair of boots two sizes too small!

I'm watching the 1st AD out of the corner of my eye for the sign but instead,

"Cut," shouts James.

I look behind me at my tribe and horror! One of them is clutching what now is a completely bald head bereft of its wig. All eyes turn skywards. Up above our heads is a huge bird circling round and round, clutching in its beak the missing article!

James jumps up and down, squawking wildly. Maybe he thinks it will make it open its beak!

"Find some food," he shouts through his megaphone.

One of the crew rushes over to the caravans and runs back with two sandwiches. James mimics the bird's flight with the sandwiches in his hands, squawking loudly. The bird doesn't respond. The bald man is clutching his head.

Suddenly, from out of nowhere, a huge gust of wind knocks the bird off its flight, it drops the wig into a muddy patch and swoops down to pick up the sandwiches.

The Hair woman holds the wig at arm's length, her other hand holding her nose.

I retire back to the Range Rover and take off my boots. I glance over to Stacey who is absorbed in her phone. She obviously has completely no interest in me. I am envious. I've exhausted every app on mine and resort to putting my headphones on and listening to music.

A while later, we're back on set, the wig now washed and cleaned and firmly positioned on the bald man's head. James reminds me of my action and we're off again.

"Cameras rolling...and...action."

I take off, charging queen-like across the moor again.

This is exhilarating. The wind whips at my face, my newly designed Eco hair flapping across my back and shoulders. I am living my part: method acting. From somewhere in the depths of my being, a spontaneous roar emerges, and my trusty tribe of warriors all join in. This is it; this why I love my job. Adrenaline pumps through my body, my heart beats like crazy, I am one with the elements and the wild windswept moors.

In my peripheral vision, I can just about see the 1st AD. His hands are flapping up and down: this is it; this is the moment for my front flip. Boy, how I'm going to impress them! The ground under my feet feels springy, just the right sort of ground to take off from. I take a running jump, bend my knees, take a deep breath and...Fuck! Fuck! Fuck! My feet in the toe crunching boots won't move. In fact, they're sinking; I can't even lift them. I am stuck in a deep muddy bog!

"Cut!"

James and the 1st AD rush towards me. James is screaming at the 1st AD and flailing his arms around like a mad thing. I grab hold of my right calf and give it an almighty pull. It won't budge, in fact it sinks into the black viscous mess even further. I try the left, no movement there either!

James and the 1st AD take hold of me under both my arms and with a big 'Heave ho' and an 'Ah' I am dragged out. James is hugely apologetic and is looking daggers at the 1st AD.

"Break for lunch."

I stumble back to the Range Rover. James is still screaming and shouting at the 1st AD whose face is now crimson. I can't quite make out what he's shouting about, but it's something about checking the ground out for bogs before deciding where the chase should take place.

Back in the car, Stacey is still absorbed in her phone. I try to start up a conversation with her.

"So, what's this film about? Who am I supposed to be chasing?"

"Posh nobs" she answers disinterestedly.

"Posh nobs?"

"They burn the heather and peat on the moors. It stimulates the growth of fresh heather which encourages red grouse to feed on it. Then they come along and shoot the birds. Causes flooding down below".

Stacey obviously knows her lines, she turns back to her phone.

"Ah, I get it, I'm chasing some posh nobs off the moor. I've never understood why people want to shoot birds, seems completely pointless to me."

"Mmmm," she doesn't even look up this time.

Full marks to James though. I'm actually rather impressed with him. So that's why they're the 'Eco-friendly film company'. This is an action-adventure movie with a serious message. I google 'grouse shooting'.

After lunch, the crew scour the moors for an alternative location and decide to shoot in the opposite direction. The Eco-Warriors are looking pretty cold now, some stamping their feet, shaking their arms, and even running up and down on the spot. I am grateful for the comfort of the Range Rover, despite having a head caked in mud, bits of which keep deciding to drop off in chunks into my eyes, my mouth and all over my clothes.

We are in position again and I jump up and down trying to shake off the dinner-time lethargy and boredom. Stacey gives me a disapproving sideways look; I smile back at her but get no response.

We're ready to go. It's my moment again, my time to impress.

"Cameras rolling…and…action."

Stacey screams her blood-curdling yell, and we charge across the moors again, my blood gushing through my veins.

"Cut!"

We stop dead. What can be the problem this time? I look round and realise one of the support actors is missing. Missing?

On these moors? As we look backwards, we hear a door swinging open and the stray Eco-warrior emerges casually from the portable toilet, adjusting his wig as he does so.

"For God's sake," shouts James, "didn't anyone notice?"

It crosses my mind that James should have been the one to have noticed. I smile and wink at the Eco-warriors around me.

"Right, first positions everyone. This time we're going for a perfect take," shouts James through his megaphone.

I take three deep breaths to try and calm my thudding heart and prepare for flight. The Eco-warriors are poised behind me.

"Cameras rolling…and…action."

Stacey does her yell and scream and we're off. I charge across the moors again with a hair-raising roar. I am at one with the wind and the elements (apart from the pesky boots!).

I keep the 1st AD in my peripheral vision as I charge. It's now, now's the time. I'm going to do it now. I don't stop, I take a deep knee-bend ready for my flight and…Oh my God! As if in slow motion my foot has caught in something, the damn thing won't move, I see myself from out of my body and…splat! I am face down, arms outstretched in front of me, mud in my eyes, up my nose, my mouth, my ears…

"Cut."

I literally can't move. My foot won't budge from whatever it's caught in. Slowly, I prise my sopping body out of the quagmire and sit up. My foot is in what appears to be a trap. I am in agony. I try to wipe some of the sopping mess from my face, scraping it off with my fingernails and wiping it with my sleeves. I start to retch; I swear there's a dead animal down there!

"You stupid, stupid man! Didn't you notice there was an effing trap?" James shouts as he runs towards me with the 1st AD, Hair and Makeup rushing behind with a bunch of towels in their hands.

"Sorry, sorry, sorry, sorry."

All I can hear in reply is the word 'sorry' over and over again.

James and the 1st AD are frantically trying to disengage my foot which is in serious danger of losing circulation. The trap won't budge, and neither will the foot. The 1st AD tries to reassure me that at least it wasn't one of the old-fashioned foothold traps. Apparently, this is a newer version, a humane trap.

"Thanks a lot, guys, that's really comforting to know! Not!"

Hair and Makeup are trying to clean the mud off my face and hair. I am getting cold. Really cold.

James shouts through his megaphone at the crew for help. They mill around me scratching their heads.

"Cut off her leg!" jokes one of them.

I fire him an exasperated look and he shrinks visibly.

"Props, fetch the toolbox," yells James.

A good half hour later, with much cutting and sawing, my now completely numb foot is finally released. James and the 1st AD help me to my feet, wrap their arms around my middle and we limp slowly back to the Hair and Makeup van, my foot hardly able to touch the ground.

Back in the van I am given two ibuprofen and a hot coffee. Many bowls of warm water, towels and hairdryers later, I am cleaned up. Life begins to come back into my injured foot which James has been nervously fussing over. He's not the only one who's worried! My errant foot has now become the focus of the whole shoot! I want to go back to Morrisons!

The light is starting to fade. There's one last chance to get this right. I limp over to my newly found first position, gritting my teeth. James is trying to look calm, but clearly isn't.

The atmosphere is tense. Really tense. Every crew member has their eyes firmly fixed on me. This has to be right.

"Cameras rolling…and…action."

I grit my teeth through the pain, take a deep breath, and remember Boadicea. Stacey does her thing.

We're off, we charge, we roar, the 1st AD waves his arms, I take a deep breath, bend my knees, propel myself up into the air and I am over, a perfect front flip.

"Cut."

My impeccable acrobatic feat is greeted by loud applause, cheers, and whistles.

"It's a wrap!"

It's a wrap for today, but do I really have to do all this again tomorrow? With this foot? Is this what defines me? Is this my soul? A stunt double to the champion of a cause I don't even believe in? But then, maybe that's all any of it is – a stunt, nothing more.

— ❧ ❧ —

The Adventures of Matty the Mouse

by Joan Watson

Connie the Caravan had been pushed into the farthest corner of the barn, and every time the door opened a cloud of dust settled all over her.

"Atishoo," sneezed Connie.

"Bless you," said a squeaky voice.

"Thank you," said Connie as four feet scampered over her top and stopped.

"My name's Matty," said the squeaky voice, "I'm a mouse. What's your name?"

"My name's Connie and I've come all the way from England."

"So have I," said Matty, "I arrived two weeks ago with another caravan."

The little mouse climbed onto an old tractor next to Connie.

"It's a long tale if you've got time to listen."

"All day, every day," said Connie in a miserable voice, "My owners have gone home and left me in this barn in France. Please tell me your story."

The little mouse tweaked his whiskers and began.

"I was born in a corn field next to a caravan park. I lived there with my father, mother, brothers and sisters. One day a big, fierce black cat called Jack came to live at the park. I enjoyed teasing Jack and one afternoon I was sent to keep him busy. He chased me all the way to the children's playground. It was fun at first, but I got trapped by him in a climbing frame."

Matty suddenly stopped talking and disappeared as one of the farm dogs started barking at the barn door.

The next day the sun beat down on the barn and Connie waited to see if Matty would come back. The barn door suddenly opened and Claude the farmer's son came in for a bale of hay. The door crashed behind him.

"Atishoo," sneezed Connie.

"Bless you," said a squeaky voice.

"Thank you," said Connie. "I am pleased to see you again. I want to know what happened next in your adventure."

"Well," said Matty, "when I escaped from Jack it started to get dark, so I looked for a safe place to spend the night. I found a small hole, crept into it and fell fast asleep. The next morning I awoke to find I was swaying and bumping along a road. I had climbed into a pipe belonging to a caravan. I went further up the pipe and crept out into a lovely warm room with crumbs on the floor and water dripping from a tap. The caravan stopped. I popped back down my pipe and found I was in another field. It was great fun. At night I would climb back up the pipe and explore the caravan. The owners heard my scratching and searched for me but couldn't find how I had got in."

Matty disappeared as the barn door creaked in the wind.

The next morning, Jeanette, the farmer's daughter came into the barn, looking for hen's eggs. When she finished, the door banged behind her.

"Atishoo," sneezed Connie.

"Bless you," said a squeaky voice.

"Thank you," said Connie. "I'm pleased to see you again. I'm curious to know what happened next in your adventure. Did you get caught?"

"No," laughed Matty, "not me! The next time I climbed down my pipe I was in a big ship crossing the sea. I had a great time exploring until a sailor caught me eating his sandwiches. He chased me up and down the stairs and I had to scamper back to my caravan."

"When we first camped in France, the owners of the caravan, Muriel and Stan, got very cross with me. Stan decided to remove the fridge to see if I was hiding behind it. I wasn't and he spent all day trying to put it back in again. He did make me laugh."

Matty looked round suddenly and said, "Bonjour Brigitte."

"What was that? I didn't understand it," said Connie.

"I said 'Bonjour.' That means 'hello' in French. I was talking to a French mouse called Brigitte."

"Bonjour Matty," said Connie with a giggle.

"Bonjour Connie," said Matty. "I must go now; I promised to get Brigitte some cheese from the dairy."

Early next morning Claude took the rusty tractor out into the farmyard, leaving clouds of dust behind him.

"Atishoo," sneezed Connie.

"Bless you," said a squeaky voice.

"Thank you," said Connie, "Tell me about your next adventure."

"Well," said Matty, "one day the caravan arrived here at this farm. The next morning, I forgot to peep out of the pipe first. Stan was peeling potatoes outside. I dropped right down in front of him. He was so startled he jumped right up and tipped over the bowl of dirty water all over his legs. He was soaked. I could hardly run for laughing. When I returned that night, Stan had blocked the pipe with paper. I couldn't get back into the caravan. That's why I live in this barn."

The barn door opened and Jeanette came in carrying a long-handled brush. She carried it over and put it beside Connie.

Connie just had time to sneeze, "Atishoo!" and for Matty to say, "Bless you!" before she returned with a bucket of water. Jeanette set to and started to scrub Connie hard. It was wonderful. All the dust and dirt came off and she was shining white again. Outside she could hear the sound of a tractor. The door opened and Claude came in.

"Bonjour, Jeanette."

"Bonjour, Claude," she replied. Jeanette walked over to talk to him and Matty followed her. He came back very quickly and told Connie that she would soon be going off on her travels to Spain.

"I've never been to Spain," said Connie excitedly.

"Neither have I," squeaked Matty, "I wonder if Brigitte fancies a holiday?"

He disappeared and Connie felt herself being pulled out into the hot sunshine. While she was being attached to the towbar she was aware of the squeaking of the two mice as they disappeared.

That night she heard Matty whispering to Brigitte, "I wonder what the Spanish is for 'Bonjour,' Brigitte?"

Shamanic Drum Circle

by Janet Griffiths

It's Monday morning and I'm sitting in my Producer's office drinking coffee and dunking Rich Tea biscuits. It's been a long weekend and I've partied hard (which I'm regretting now as I do every Monday morning!). My Producer also doesn't look 'as fresh as a daisy' (to coin an expression).

He isn't giving anything away, but I can tell by the hints he gave me last Friday that he's got something interesting in store.

"Okay, Kate, the next programme we're going to make is going to look at New Age spiritual practices which are becoming more and more popular these days and we've located a little town in West Yorkshire where a lot of these practices are taking place. We'd like to send you on a mission this week to find out what you can, try a few out, who knows you might even come back a different person....spiritually enlightened!"

And he sits back in his large Producer's office chair and staring at me laughs.

"What's so funny, boss?" I ask.

"You...spiritually enlightened!" and he laughs again.

I'm thinking the same thing and soon we're both rolling around laughing hysterically. Well, I am only a working class girl from Salford, I think, but this mission sounds interesting.

"So where is this town in West Yorkshire where all this stuff goes on," I ask.

"It's called Hebden Bridge....you might have heard of it. It was taken over by hippies in the 70s and never lost its reputation," he replies.

"So what sort of stuff goes on there?" I enquire.

"Well, Kate, that's what we want you to find out. Bound to be lots of yoga, so go and pack your bag, take your yoga mat, we've booked you a nice little place for the week, good luck and we'll see you on the other side."

So now I'm on the train trying to Google what's on in Hebden Bridge. As we head further and further from Salford, the landscape becomes quite beautiful, big hills, rock formations, fields and loads of trees. Yoga, yoga and more yoga! I stumble across the Calderdale Yoga Centre website, loads of classes: Hatha yoga, Vinyasa flow and what's this? Kundalini yoga. What on earth is Kundalini yoga? I decide to start it and see if I can find out. I've done a few yoga classes in my time but no-one's ever talked about Kundalini yoga. Apparently, according to the blurb it cleans out your chakras (Chakras what are my chakras, I've never heard of them!) and allows your kundalini to rise, bringing spiritual healing and awareness. Ooooh that sounds really funky. Can't wait!

I find a sound healing gong bath, that sounds wacky, gotta go to that, a sweat lodge (hmmm not sure about that one, don't fancy having to get naked if that's what you have to do) and countless therapists offering all sort of weird sounding treatments: 'access consciousness bars', 'heal your inner child' 'soul retrieval'... well, I've had a few massages but nothing like these!

But what's this – a Shamanic drum circle and it's on tonight! Well that's definitely my first mission.

Hebden Bridge is lovely, I like it already, can't see many hippies around but there's a lot of new age types.

After settling myself in my cute little holiday flat, I head out on to the town to find some dinner…got a couple of hours to kill before my first encounter with the 'spiritual world'. A lot of the restaurants seem to be vegan or vegetarian, but I'm starving so I stumble into a burger bar…can't go wrong with a burger!

I could die for a gin and tonic, my nerves are a bit on edge, probably due to the anticipation, but decide in the circumstances it's probably not a good idea at this stage.

The Shamanic drum circle is up a big hill, a really steep hill, so steep I have to stop several times before I reach the Roydcliffe centre and I stumble through the door panting, wheezing and sweating!

I'm met by a very tall man with long black wavy hair and a grey beard. He's dressed in a green tunic with baggy Ali baba pants and beads around his neck.

"Welcome, do come in, my name's Sam."

I guess he's the Shamanic leader.

The room is dimly lit with candles, smells strongly of incense and another strange smell I don't recognise. There are several people sitting in a circle on cushions, looking serene and relaxed. Some even have their eyes closed – meditating, I suppose. I feel far from serene; in fact, now I look round, I'm not sure about this at all.

"Would you like to be saged?" Sam asks.

Saged, what does he mean by 'saged', I wonder.

"Umm, yes, okay," I answer, wanting to find out more about saging.

"It cleanses all your negative energies and prepares you for the healing to take place," Sam explains.

I stand there while he takes the sage stick out of a saucer, lights it and passes its burning stick all over me, front and back. I'm not sure whether I like the smell at all, but I stand there attempting to look serene like the others.

After the saging, I plump myself down between two people who both look quite friendly, they turn to smile at me. Sam moves round everyone in the room, handing out little instruments…I get a rattle.

"While we're waiting for others to come and the circle to begin, let's sit in silent meditation," Sam suggests to us.

The room is deathly quiet except for the sounds of more shamanic people coming in to join us and getting 'saged' in readiness for whatever is going to happen.

Meditation! I haven't got a clue on how to meditate, I tried staring at a candle once, as suggested in a Facebook post, but it only made my eyes sore and watery. My thoughts are chasing themselves round and round in my head; I don't know about meditating, all I can think about is what I did at the weekend: *Oh my God, I didn't, did I? Oh no….* Round and round my thoughts go. I'm completely useless at this.

Suddenly, from out of nowhere, my stomach starts to rumble. Not only rumble, but gurgle as well. Oh, no! How embarrassing. On and on it goes….as soon as it stops, it starts again, like an orchestra going off in my belly. I can see people out of the corner of my eye looking at me... cringe, oh cringe... but I'm powerless to stop it. Must have been that burger and chips I had, obviously the wrong thing to eat before a shamanic drum circle. Should have gone for the vegan option! On and on it goes, rumble, gurgle, pop. *Stop, stop,* I want to scream, but on and on it goes.

"Now it's time for our intention," Sam explains, "Who wants to go first?"

My intention? What is my intention? I can't tell them I'm a researcher from a TV programme!

I listen while people talk about blocked chakras, releasing blocked emotional patterns, wanting to connect with their spirit helpers, connect with power animals. When it gets to my turn, I quickly mutter something about wanting to de-stress and heal...heal from what I'm not sure, but it sounds good!

Sam picks up his rattle and starts to dance round the room, everyone follows shaking their instruments and dancing around. I feel like I'm back in Modern Educational Dance at school and almost break out in embarrassed laughter, but somehow manage to dance into a corner and suppress it before anyone sees.

Sam turns to me and says, "We're clearing the space of negative energies before the journey."

Journey, what journey, what does me mean about a journey...are we going to go somewhere? I wonder.

After some time, which does seem to go on for quite a long time, this dancing around and clearing the negative energies, everyone sits down in the circle again and Sam tells us it's now time for 'the journey'.

"Can I suggest as you're a newcomer, you journey to the lower realms, not the higher realms as they are more advanced to reach," he explains.

What does he mean by the lower realms? He can evidently see I'm looking quizzical, so he tells me to imagine I'm sitting under a favourite tree and I'm to go inside the tree for the journey.

Well, if he insists! We all lie down and cover ourselves with blankets and eye masks and Sam begins to drum on a flattish circular drum with feathers hanging off the sides, softly and rhythmically at first, then louder and louder.

I desperately try to imagine myself inside a tree, I don't have a favourite tree, there aren't many in Salford, but I try to conjure one up.

I'm inside the tree but I'm stuck! The drumming is hypnotic and quite exciting, but I feel far from relaxed. Into my mind, from nowhere comes a vision, a vision of when I was stuck in a cave when I went potholing with the school as a teenager (not an experience I would have preferred to remember!) It's black, totally black, my light's gone out, I can't see anything, I can't hear anything, everyone's gone on ahead and I am rooted to the spot not daring to move. I'm screaming hysterically for help, terrified that if I move, I'll fall into a deep cavern. I can hear a teacher coming towards me…

You stupid girl, just put your our feet down you're only six inches from the ground! Oh, the shame!

The drumming starts to slow down, gets quieter and quieter until it eventually stops. The vision of the cave is stuck in my mind.

"And now it's time for sharing," Sam tells us.

I listen as once again people talk about opening their blocked chakras, cleansing emotional blocks, finding spirit animals etc and I dread my turn!

I tell Sam and the group about the vision of the cave and how terrified I felt.

"That's good," Sam says, "you obviously needed to restore the vibrational integrity of mind, body and spirit," and he smiles benevolently at me.

For my part, I feel like a nervous wreck as I stumble down the hill to sort my chakras out another way with a large gin and tonic!

DNA

by Alison Milner

"Old age ain't for sissies."

Grandma likes to think she has Bette Davis eyes and often quotes her icon.

We're in a deserted Calder Valley mill. There's a strong smell of lanolin and donkey stone.

Grandma appears in her blue overalls in the centre of a vast weaving shed. In one corner are the two toddlers she left behind, eyes wide, hair uncombed. Beside them the baby who left her, looking like a peeled prawn.

"We picked up that smashed jam jar. It took us ages to pick out all the splinters of glass. But what a treat. Jammy fingers, mixed with only the slightest smear of blood."

"Time for tea."

A polished oak table shimmers in a searchlight of sun and solidifies. It is set for six. Bone china crockery, patterned with purple wisteria.

I must be invited because suddenly I'm sitting with the other guests round the table. Grandma, Nana, Nana's third husband Walt, and the two children from the corner, who tell me shyly their names are Dad and Auntie.

"Walt's lost his leg," Nana says reproachfully.

She points to his walking stick. Nana's forgotten she lost her real name, birthdate and first marriage certificate deliberately, before unconsciously, losing her marbles. Miniature glass balls scatter and roll, spinning out of control.

Nana says, "I'll have lemon drizzle cake. The zesty yellow matches my twin set."

The children both choose chocolate sponge.

Dad says, "I don't like marzipan."

I finally understand why the icing snow on childhood Christmas cakes was always slightly muddy beneath small plastic Santa's boots.

Walt and Grandma decide on Battenberg, even though they both agree it's a shame such a peculiarly British confection has a German name.

I look at the slice of Battenburg on my plate. The pastel pink and vanilla squares make me feel queasy. DNA bricks, mortared by marzipan and jam blood.

The tea steams, strong and aromatic. Grandma says she doesn't think there will be time to read the leaves. Auntie mutters that only fools want to see their future.

I hear the clock chiming, but I know it's not midnight yet. No need to dash. It's still light. A radio alarm flashes neon. I'm supposed to be meeting a friend for coffee in an hour! I think I'll give the cake a miss this morning.

Coach Trip

by Roy Greenwood

"You're a coach party aren't you," demanded the frosty, plump, middle-aged woman behind the bar as she pulled the third pint of beer.

By now, the 15 of us that were left on the trip had drifted casually into the pub's 'high class' atmosphere in twos and threes.

I and my three companions looked hurt.

"We're all together, but we came in cars," I lied.

"I think you're a coach party," she replied, but continued to pull the beer while other bar staff served the rest of our party.

I passed a pint to Roger. He took a swig and grimaced.

"Christ it tastes about as bloody good as she looks," he whispered, indicating the woman behind the bar.

We looked and burst out laughing. The woman stood no higher than five feet, with probably the same measurement round the waist. She wore a blue polo neck jumper and tight black trousers. She looked like a sack of potatoes tied at both ends with a face to match said Josh.

She gave us the sort of stare that would have turned many a lesser – or more sober – mortal to stone. We carried on laughing. What the hell, we were miles from home on a rugby club trip.

As we downed our first pint, we all agreed the beer tasted foul, so we had another. Again the frosty reaction from the frump behind the bar. She knew we had come by coach, but as we had parked it a hundred yards away round a bend, she couldn't prove it – a tactic we had used so successfully on other major campaigns in 'no coaches land'.

But as we were the only ones in the pub – it was only 7.15pm on a Saturday night – we felt we were doing them a favour.

Basically, it was a sort of plastic palace. It must have obviously been a fairly old building, but inside it had the sort of imitation wooden beams that you can tell a mile off are false.

We were a bit noisy, but we were not causing any trouble – except for Big Joe. Although now 45, Joe stood 6ft 6in, weighed about 20 stone and was as tough as an undercooked piece of gristly steak. All the time he had been muttering that he was not prepared to be treated like a second-class citizen. Why should he pretend he hadn't come on a coach?

Finishing our drinks, we decided to move on. Just then, the fat woman came out from behind the bar.

"Right lads, let's get back on t'bus," shouted Dave.

She stood there and watched us all go out. Dave was the last to leave.

"I knew you were a coach party," she told him triumphantly.

"But we didn't cause any bother, did we?" he said.

"Just remember next time no coaches," she answered ushering him through the door.

Bowing low he replied in his best W. C. Fields voice, "Lady there won't be no next time."

All in all, it was well-behaved trip and a strange one in a way for most of the regulars were missing. There were a few veterans like myself. At 35 we must have seemed ancient to the youngsters who were enjoying their first 'stopping trip.'

There are two kinds of 'stopping trip' – either you travel from area to area stopping at pubs along the way as we were doing, or you stay firmly in one town, like the night we invaded Wetherby. Invasion being the right term as we hit every pub in the town in a mass drinking orgy.

But this time we were well behaved. We veterans even tut-tutted when one younger member emerged from one pub with three glasses and a small pot plant. This was soon followed with much-embellished tales of how various items were acquired from hostelries up and down the country. In particular, there was the much-told and much-laughed-at story of how 'Conny', annoyed at a landlord's attitude, casually removed a full-size javelin from the pub, although what the javelin was doing there in the first place and exactly how he got it out still remain a mystery.

But soon it was time for the all-important ritual which plays a major role in every trip – letting nature play its course in the most unlikely spot, or as it is more popularly known the 'piss stop.'

The more unlikely the spot, the greater the challenge. But let's face it, when you're desperate anywhere will do. Still, at the side of a busy road into Manchester was quite an achievement, especially as a passing police car did not seem to pay much attention – and the coach was parked on a double yellow line.

After the relief, it was time for more laughter as the old tales came out again for the benefit of the younger members – the saga of Dennis and his motor bike, the York disco battle, big Joe's 5am visit to Swansea hospital and the hotel that banned us twice.

Time for another, this time at a scruffy-looking little pub where the driver assured us there was a fantastic pint of beer. It was small, drab and dreary, but full of life. Our reception was warm – it's funny how the small places always seem happy to see parties like ours.

But we only stopped for one drink as the beer did not quite live up to the driver's description, in fact, as Dave put it, it was only worth squirting up a certain part of his anatomy – or words to that effect.

Back on the bus it was time for a few more stories and the odd song or two as we began to near Halifax. As there was still a good hour of drinking time left before the bus had to be back, we decided to call at a regular haunt, one where we had always been welcome. After all, we did have something to celebrate, having travelled away into foreign climes – Lancashire – and beaten the buggers.

The Devil at the End of the Bed

by Janet Griffiths

He only comes out when it's dark, completely dark, pitch black, dense blackness, blackness that I can't even see through. I know he's there tonight because it's the darkest I have ever seen it, (if that's the right word) because I can't see anything at the moment. Blackness, deep dark blackness.

I can hear him breathing. I'm sure I can, a kind of hoarse type of breathing, not a human kind of breathing. And now I can hear my own breath. I'm not aware that I can usually hear my own breath, but I certainly can now. Two sounds, the sound of his hoarse breath and the sound of my breath getting quicker and quicker.

And now there's another sound I can hear, a thud, thud, thud, where's that coming from? I can't tell in the darkness, but I don't like it.

I touch myself; I touch my body all over to make sure I'm still alive, I sure am, I'm warm all over under my nightie. I feel my heart, it's definitely beating, so that's where the thudding noise is coming from, from my own heart!

I shiver and shudder and sit up in my bed. I pull my dressing gown around me to keep myself warm.

The hoarse breathing is getting louder and I don't like it, I really don't like it, I don't like it one bit!

I close my eyes and put my hands together in front of my chest. Perhaps if I said my prayers like I used to, the horrible hoarse breathing will stop!

"Our Father who art in heaven."

The Knock-on Effect

by Chris Freeman

I heard the sound long before I knew what was coming. It began as a background whine, but quickly grew to a deafening pitch, such that I had to seek shelter from it. Even when I was in my home and well away from the cool fresh air of the day, I could still feel the sound biting into my brain. Then suddenly it stopped and welcome relief spread through my body and I began to relax for the first time in quite a while. I looked over at my partner lying next to me; she was sick, but I couldn't let her know that I knew she was.

We needed to eat, so I went out into the night to see what was about and what I saw sent a shiver down my spine. There in the mist was a huge craft, the like of which I had never seen before. The red buses that carried so many people were nothing compared to this monster and I just stared at the enormity of it. Dark grey in the night, it had odd little lights around the edge and as I watched it, a faint whistle began to pervade my being. The noise was as if it was actually in my head and then I heard the voices. Not seen, just heard, inside my head. I turned away from the craft, but the strange voices were still there in my head, filling my brain with some unheard of language. I was drawn to look back at the craft and then transfixed, I watched as an opening appeared high up on the side of the craft and a blinding light filled the darkness of the night. So bright was the light that the creatures that emerged were surrounded by pure light and they just floated, without steps or other support, and gracefully descended to the ground.

As the blinding light faded, I could see that the creatures were holding on to something like a hose that was also attached to the craft and they seemed to float at the end of the hose and move outwards as they did. The sight was so mesmerising that at first I didn't hear the new sound that came with the creatures. A whistling sound that was much higher pitched than before and only just audible, even to me. I sensed an acute danger and instinctively ran full tilt back to my home and dived into the darkness to snuggle down safely next to my partner.

A very strange and unpleasant odour began to percolate down to us, and we instinctively moved away from it, closing down as we did so. We were both still hungry, but the best thing for us to do was to sleep and conserve our energy. My partner breathed uneasily and every now and again, she would jerk and cough and I knew then that she was getting worse. We desperately needed food, but our safety was the most important thing now.

I awoke at the same time that I awoke every day and for a moment, forgot about the trauma of last night. As I stirred, so did my partner and we looked at each other in the darkness, not able to see each other, but both knowing what we were doing. Instinct is a wonderful thing, but I soon remembered, as my stomach was telling me quite obviously, that we needed food.

I scrambled out towards the dim daylight of dawn and could immediately smell the faint smell that had been so much stronger the night before. As my eyes grew accustomed to the light, I could see the alien creatures all around, picking up dead animals and putting them into some kind of translucent sacks.

There were people too, lying everywhere and they too were being scooped up. My brain raced. Close by there were dead animals; could I grab one and not be noticed? Would they be safe to eat, as the creatures had obviously gassed them the night before?

I took a chance and stealthily moved closer to a dead pheasant and just had time to pick it up and run for cover. As I ran, there it was again, those strange voices in my head. Within a second or so the voices became tuned to my own language and they bade me to stop or else, but I ran on and dived for cover, out of site and into safety.

Triumphant, I sat down next to my partner and offered the pheasant to her, but she was motionless and I knew, in my heart, that I was too late to say goodbye to my lifelong love. Suddenly, the pheasant was not important and I had the horrible realisation that I too may suffer the same fate as her.

I slept for a while, but soon woke up to the rumblings of my stomach. This time I ate the pheasant to quell my hunger. There was still a faint smell of the gas, but I was too hungry to bother whether it was safe or not.

Tucked away, out of sight, I felt safe, but I soon became aware of the voices in my head again and this time they were speaking my language. They couldn't find me though and I stayed motionless in case they could hear my movements. They soon moved off and I went on with the task of finishing my meal, but I was ever conscious of my poor dead partner close by.

With my belly full, I drifted into a half sleep and then it came to me. If those creatures could speak to me, in my head, could I speak to them in the same way? Could they hear me speak, even if I was only thinking? My crafty inner being began to work out a cunning plan and as with all good plans, the best thing to do is to sleep on it.

My body clock instinctively woke me at dusk and I moved carefully and without any complete thought in my head, toward the smell of fresh air. I had managed to hypnotise myself into having an empty brain, so that if my feet made no noise, neither did my brain. I was invisible if I was quiet. As I moved out towards the craft I saw several of the beings moving around and the strange way that they moved told me that they really must be of the animal world. Now within a few yards of the creatures I started to allow my mind to fill with the kindest thoughts that I could. Warm, generous thoughts, of the sort that one sends to one's partner in intimate situations. As I got close to one of the creatures, it turned to look at me and I instinctively lay down and looked up at it, all the time, telling it, and myself, that I was really only a friend that wanted to help.

The creature came to me and as it did I licked its leg and what passed for a hand, all the time giving out the kindest, warmest thoughts that I could. Soon other creatures joined us and they too were falling under my spell and receiving the same fawning treatment from me. I was slowly winning them over and I knew that I would ultimately win this war. As I lifted my head, one of them actually bowed down to kiss me and I knew that I really had won!

Still thinking kindest thoughts, I moved away and went back to my home, picking up another dead pheasant on the way.

I stayed low for several days now, resting and waiting. Although I had eaten plenty, I too began to feel unwell so on the third day I made the decision that I had to see what was happening outside.

It would normally have been a dangerous time to venture out, as there was still plenty of light and it was well before dusk, but the sight that greeted me filled my heart with joy. Not only could I see the dead animals that the creatures had gassed, but there were also plenty of the alien creatures lying on the ground and most were writhing in agony.

I move amongst the creatures and now my thoughts were of hatred and loathing, but they could do nothing as they were obviously in great pain and were suffering. I could hear their voices, but they were muffled and strange. As I moved about I began to hear the voice of their leader, weakly calling to me and I moved closer to the massive craft.

"Save us. What is happening to us?" the creature begged.

"You are all dying from a terrible disease!" I said in my most cocky way.

"You think that you can come here, to our planet and take it over, as your own? You are sadly mistaken!"

The pitiful creature staggered forwards and looked me straight in the eye.

"What have you done to us?" it begged.

I looked at the pathetic sight before me.

"You are dying and so am I," I told it. "My partner is dead and I will die soon, but so will all of you!"

I turned and walked slowly away, my own strength beginning to fade too, but I was proud of what I had done.

There was one last thought from the creature that came into my head, "What disease have you given us?"

"No chance my friend. If I tell you, then you can pass the knowledge to the rest of your kind, so you will die in ignorance."

"Who are you?" begged the creature, but it was too late.

As its head went down I knew they were all gone. I too would soon be gone, so I made my way back to my partner and as I lay my head on her chest, my thoughts drifted.

"My partner caught it, I caught it and now the aliens have caught it. That's the knock-on effect and rabies is a terrible disease for anyone to suffer."

With that thought, I closed my eyes for the last time and as I too faded away, I shouted for the last time, "I am the last urban fox."

The Journey

by Janet Griffiths

It's day five of my journey. Arriving in Mytholmroyd, I've already covered a hundred miles and there's many more to go. My feet are so sore, I've had to cover the blisters with plasters, I can still feel them, but I'm trying to ignore the pain. My spirits are high, it's a beautiful sunny day, and as I look up into the blue azure of the sky, I can see fluffy white clouds floating by and long trails of white feathery trails formed by aeroplanes flying high overhead.

Everywhere looks so green, the leaves on the trees, the bushes, the plants and weeds that I pass, interspersed with some of the leaves and plants just starting to change with the season into beautiful golds, yellows, oranges and reds. Some of them have already died and have created a brown blanket on the stony path which makes a crunching sound as I walk. Molly trots along ahead of me, her paws creating crisp crackling sounds, stopping every now and again when she finds a new smell to sniff, or when she squats down for a wee which creates a puddle on the ground.

The river to my right is rushing and gurgling over stones and boulders, making a constant sound and creating a white froth in places. I sit down on a bench and Molly trots down to the water for a paddle; plop, plop, plop goes the water as she splashes around happily in the water, her tail wagging madly,.

Across the other side of the river I can see three children swinging on a rope, their voices calling to each other and laughing. In the distance a lawn mower hums in a field.

As I sit, I contemplate. I am journeying to forget, forget what has happened, forgetting to mend the past which has not been kind to me. With every step I take the trauma is fading and I am healing.

Molly trots back up from the river and we continue walking. To my left is a perfect green field, apart from the odd brown earthy mole hill and I take in the delicious smell of freshly mown grass. On the far side of the field lies a large, discarded rusty roller, and I spot the man who had been mowing the grass sitting on a tree stump taking a rest and drinking out of a thermos flask.

A friendly lady passes me and we have a brief conversation about how lovely the weather is and how the sun is just about to fade behind the hill behind us. But at the moment, the sunlight is still sparkling on the water in the river and the coloured leaves are still on the trees.

Eventually, we come to a small river beach where I sit down between two big old trees with roots like fingers which bury themselves deep into the earth below. This place feels damp, I can feel a dampness on my hands and face. Molly lies down beside me on the sandy floor to take a rest. Here the river is calmer, as it flows gently along and meanders around rocks. On the other side of the river are many tall thin trees; the sunlight casts their shadows onto a large, old stone wall.

I close my eyes and he comes into my mind. I wish he wouldn't. I really wish he wouldn't! I don't want to see his face, hear his voice, be reminded.

To try and distract myself, I prise myself up and find a stick for Molly to swim for.

"Walk," I tell myself, "Just keep walking, try and let his image float by like one of the fluffy white clouds in the sky, don't cling on!"

We walk past an allotment with makeshift buildings built with old doors and windows, surrounded by an old wire fence, past an enormous tree that's fallen down, past the river which is now rushing over boulders making a deafening sound, past a couple, one on a phone, past some rocky crags and as we do, I can feel the wind on my face and arms and hear birds singing and tweeting above, sounding so sweet.

We come to an old metal bridge over the river covered in moss. We don't cross the bridge but take the path to the left and as I check the map wedged into my pocket, I realise I have reached our destination for the night.

I search around and find a flat piece of land, where I pitch my tent for the night. Hidden from view, underneath a hawthorn bush whose berries have all dropped off and whose remaining leaves are turning black and curly. There are goosebumps on my skin as the sun fades and I search around for some wood to make a fire with. My sore feet are so grateful as I gently warm them.

One more day on my journey, one more day of forgetting!

Toys

by Roy Greenwood

It was his favourite toy. Ever since he had found it, all his other playthings seemed somehow inadequate. It kept him enthralled time after time in the way nothing else ever did.

It had happened quite by chance. He had come across this new toy as he had wandered idly around. His mother had grown tired of him hanging about and told him to go find something to play with.

Now he could see the star in the distance and quickly he glided toward it. He passed millions of other stars, but he was not interested in them. He reached the star, circled it slowly and then moved off to his favourite toy – the third orbiting sphere.

With excitement mounting, he settled his presence around the sphere and opened his mind to what was going on down there on that small world – his world.

No one had a toy as good as his. He had boasted about it so much that they had all tried to make him tell where it was. But he had stubbornly refused, determined to let it remain his secret. He did not want anything to spoil his fun.

And he had so nearly passed it by. Just those few simple thought waves had attracted his attention as he had wandered idly close to the sphere. But he had been bored and his curiosity got the better of him. It was then that he discovered his world and the strange little creatures who spent their short lives there.

He remembered how at first he had settled nearby and merely watched. Then he had moved closer for some reason and focused his whole being on one of them.

As he concentrated, he suddenly realised he could sense the thought waves emanating from the little creature.

His attention was completely fixed and as he studied with the whole of his presence he became aware that he could put his thoughts into the creature's mind. He became the creature. He could sense the feel of its body. It was such fun.

Then he found he could move the creature's body. What a strange sensation – it was something he had never experienced before. He watched other creatures moving and found he could make his own creature move along in the same way on two of its longer appendages. But it had fallen off the edge of a piece of the world.

He had moved the various parts of the body as it fell, but nothing had happened. When it hit the bottom he felt slight stab of pain – but it wasn't pain – it was… Well he didn't really know what it was, except that he liked it. He tried to move the body, but it would not. So he abandoned it and turned his attention elsewhere.

Later he found he could move into the minds of several of the creatures at one time. He made them do all kinds of things, but mainly he enjoyed making them fight each other. He enjoyed the hurting and being hurt.

The more he played, the more ways he found to receive that slight stab of pain – no pleasure – as another creature's body became useless.

He soon got to like his little toys and the pleasure they gave him. He found they had names too and some of them he liked so much, he stayed with them for some time. It was fun to see them trying to destroy each other – mainly on impulses sent to them from him.

He thought about some of the times he had enjoyed and some of the creatures he had taken over. He remembered their names – names like Adolf Hitler and Lee Harvey Oswald.

There had been a time too when he had decided to try a different approach. That had been after a lecture from his mother. She had scolded him and it had had an effect on him.

He went back to his world, looked at his creatures, and, after some thought, decided to try to make the creatures care about each other. He would use one of them as an example to the others. He remembered the creature's name – Jesus. He persevered, but somehow it just wasn't as much fun. Then he heard his mother calling to him and ended his experiment.

Now, however, he had plenty of time. It had taken him a while to escape from his friends this time, but finally he had done it. They had no idea where his toys were and anyway he always took a different route to reach the star.

He was here now, and he was determined to enjoy himself. He sent his presence ranging all over the sphere, searching, searching. Soon he made up his mind, and thinking of all the fun he would have, he focused his being on to one of the creatures. Reaching out he started to move into a new mind.

There was no reaction. The creature never felt anything. But soon it realised there was something it had to do and prepared itself, waiting for nightfall.

Slipping stealthily from the rear of his house he made his way through the suburbs of a place named Belfast. Crouching in the shadow of a wall he sprung, catching the soldier off guard.

With a quick thrust, the knife went into his back and the soldier slid gurgling to the ground. The man grabbed the machine gun from the dead soldier's hands and ran off, ignoring the bullets which spattered against the walls around him.

The following day he took the gun and moved into a position from which he could watch the Royal route...

North Light

by Alison Milner

A wing, as light as tissue paper, strokes my cheek. A brush of feathers, gentle but strangely sinister, ghostly in the cavernous interior blackened by the harsh dazzle of the sunlight outside.

A papier-mâché heron, clerical grey, cloaked, beak bowed as if in prayer, swings like a hanged man above my head, circling slowly in the breeze from the open mill door. My eyes, a pin hole camera, focus. Fantasy riots around me. A world of magic unveils itself, akin to dust covers being removed flamboyantly by a butler in a shrouded stately home preparing for a grand re-opening.

The long rectangular hall houses the art of the Handmade Parade. Cardboard creatures, mythological and natural, bonded by glue and wire and wishful thinking. They crowd the floor, float on long silken cords, or sway on braided rope suspended from the barrelled ceiling.

Like Alice, I am lost in a land of wonder. My sight adjusts to the darkness, but my other senses do not. They dance, flirting with perception. Colours have aromas, shadows shift key.

I tread carefully through a paper lily pond, trying not to crease the waxy kidney-shaped leaves or damage the delicate cupped flowers, petals spiralling in pink and white. Their yellow stigma wave, small candle flames flickering in glass vortex holders.

Bright green frogs, startled, watch me warily. An owl's head swivels on a stick, black eyes glinting amid tawny ruffles. A giant parade puppet with a sharp pointed nose leers at me. His lolling head drunk, his many long strings a tangled web.

A framed notice, pinned next to a picture of a big top, is entitled RULES in bold red capital letters. 'No words, no logos.' It is an instruction not an exhortation.

"I agree that this is art of the object." The voice echoes, pistol shots in the vast silent space. "A strange sentiment for a poet. Apprentice poet," he corrects himself hastily.

"I'm creating a bear. He's big and grisly. I want to show him to you."

The voice has a pale, etched face and moonstone blue eyes.

"I haven't introduced myself. I'm Henry. I'm one of the Handmade Parade."

"Anna," I say, but I'm speaking to his back as he strides quickly down the narrow aisle between racks of inert puppets.

"Come on," he urges, "My studio is here."

He stops before an archway on the rear wall of the room. My feet follow his, ignoring the hesitation in my head. By the time I pass through the doorway, he's already climbing a steep flight of metal stairs. I grasp the cold handrail, trying not to look through the wide, open treads which patina the stairwell with sliced fluorescent light.

At the top of the stairs is a square room with large rectangular windows running the entire length of one wall.

Despite this, the light is mellow, the room warm but not hot on this day pulsating with heat.

"North light, in a northern hemisphere summer," Henry says, "an artist's dream."

"My studio catches seasons in cusp," he continues, looking at a large tree, its trunk made from corrugated cardboard, bark roughly painted chestnut brown. Crisp matt leaves in a lighter buff shade droop like horseshoe bats from its branches.

"Coffee," he says, but it isn't a question as the filled kettle is already boiling noisily, snorting plumes of wispy steam into the air.

He pulls a heavy office chair, screeching on its castors, towards me. The seat is covered by worn upholstery in a mustard yellow so strong it stings. A sweep of his arm indicates I should sit, and I do, my legs dangling.

"I'm repairing them," he says as I stare at the tangle of broken puppets sprawled in a heap. Their painted eyes gaze back devoid of expression, but their contorted mouths and awkwardly angled limbs express pain.

"Gosh, that's a big job," I say lamely. "A skilled job, lots of intricate work."

"It's a labour of love." He smiles, his teeth glinting small and sharp.

"This is Boris."

The torso of a bear squats on its haunches. It is the size of a large person, with chunks of fur stuck onto its wire mesh frame, creating a mottled coat. Alongside it sit four paws covered in black hair with white claws curving like sickles. Paws so life-like that their dismemberment appears grotesque.

"You can stroke him. He's soft."

I approach cautiously, but my hands are caressed by the silky fur. It feels real.

"It wasn't easy or cheap to collect the fur," Henry says, "Boris is dressed in the skins of many mammals, long since deceased, from a time before animal rights influenced fashion."

"I haven't started the head," he says. "I can't decide whether Boris should be grinning or growling. It depends on my mood. Actually, it rather depends on you. Will you have dinner with me this weekend?"

Suddenly it seems very important that the bear should be friendly, benign, a fitting childhood companion.

My lips move like a ventriloquist's dummy, "Yes, why not?"

I'm uncomfortably warm as I enter the restaurant but the tables outside, their red cloths fluttering at the edges, are already taken. Henry is sat at the back of the dining room, studying his mobile phone. I check my watch, but I'm not late.

He smiles as I approach.

"Anna," he stands, as if announcing my entrance to a grand occasion. "I've made some progress with Boris. He's acquired more fur since you saw him."

I'm glad to sit on the chair he's pulled out. My legs feel jerky.

"Good," I hear myself say, "Does he have a deadline?"

"No, not particularly."

He seems disinterested and I wonder what on earth we'll talk about during the course of an entire dinner.

"I recommend the trout, with samphire. That's what I'm having."

Henry says this as he hands me a menu which is of a size to shield my face. The italic letters dance and I'm overwhelmed by the elaborate description of the dishes.

"I'll have the same as you," my voice sounds oddly conciliatory.

I have no idea what samphire is, but its name intrigues me.

Henry removes his navy cloth cap, revealing a glancing frown before his black hair flops over his heavy eyebrows. He waves his cap in the air and a waiter appears on cue.

"We'll both have the trout please and a bottle of Picpoul. Could you tell the chef the trout's for me?"

The samphire, which is the same colour and texture as the green plastic plants sold for tropical fish tanks, is delicious. Salt marshes stretch, smelling of the sea, as pink flesh is flaked from my crisply baked trout. Henry's fish is paler and spineless.

"You mentioned you write poetry?" I'm not feigning an interest now.

"Yes, but I don't like to talk about it. It's not good. It embarrasses me."

"Free verse or rhyme?" I persist.

"Right on both counts. Prose poetry."

The conversation is cut, neatly severed from the bone, like the fish.

Henry is eating quickly, his utensils flashing like toy swords in the flickering light of the tea candle placed in the centre of our table. I focus on my table manners.

"Picpoul has to be drunk as young as possible," Henry says pouring himself another glass, "It fades fast."

I take another sip of my wine. It's dry and vivid, zesty with citrus.

"How long have you been involved with the Handmade Parade?"

"Only a couple of years, but I've been a puppeteer for ever."

Henry is animated now and waves his empty fork in the air like a conductor's baton.

"Marionettes. Such a proud tradition. My father left me his Victorian puppet theatre. It's beautiful, intricate and ornate, yet portable, practical. You must see it, it's at my house."

Thankfully, Henry stays seated, I am only halfway through my dinner and I'm not sure I want to visit his home.

"Chaucer uses the word puppet." I say, with more confidence than I feel.

"Yes, in Canterbury Tales the host describes Geoffrey the pilgrim as 'a popet in an arm t'embrace.' Popet may just mean doll, of course, but I bet there were puppets in fourteenth century England."

"I loved Sooty and Sweep when I was a kid."

Henry looks irritated so I change the subject again.

"Why do you call the bear Boris?"

"It's a good outlet for my anger. A devil is riding bare backed across the central plains of our continent."

Henry places his hands heavily on the table and the wine bottle, now empty, wobbles.

"We cannot verify lies are not truth, images are not fake, democracy is not dictatorship in war," he states. "Propaganda punctures the news like the beak of a great carrion bird."

"I assume you'll want a desert?"

Henry's question sounds like an accusation, so I decline politely.

"We'll settle the bill when I come back," I say as I flee for the bathroom.

"The bill is already sorted. I've ordered a taxi for you; it may already be parked outside," Henry calls after me.

Henry is waiting for me beside the exit when I return. He's now wearing a smart, long black coat over his immaculate white shirt. I notice he is wearing black leather cowboy boots.

Henry follows me out of the restaurant into the gathering grain of dusk. He strides purposefully towards a hackney cab and opens the door for me with a theatrical bow. The driver is wearing a peaked hat and thick glasses. Henry looks at me quizzically as he closes the door.

"7 Queen's Terrace," I say and the vehicle glides smoothly into the night.

Henry's invitation arrives amid a flutter of junk mail. I do not recognise the spidery handwriting. I pick up the red envelope gingerly. It's glued down firmly, but when I manage to slice it open with a flat kitchen knife I'm charmed by its contents.

On a piece of thick drawing paper is a skilfully detailed sketch of a Victorian puppet theatre finished in oil pastel. It has two white Corinthian columns supported on a plinth decorated with a gold ivy motif. The crimson velvet curtains are drawn back to reveal a woodland stage set, a beige path curving through leafy trees which diminish in size until they vanish into a sunlit distance.

The words on the invitation are starkly minimal in contrast to the lavish image, 'Saturday 6th, 18.00, 6 New Delight. Food and a performance. Hope it's a convenient time for you.'

There is no RSVP.

It's a wild, wet evening, large rain drops splattering like glass beads from a broken chain as I board the bus in town. There are only two other passengers nestled into the bright seats, garish under artificial light. The bus growls, low gears grating, as it climbs the steep valley side, up and onto the tops.

The moors are mottled brown like an ancient hand; knuckle contours a clenched fist. Our fifteen-minute journey slices a world living between the breathing of peat and the rasping of blackened heather.

The shrieking wind is silenced suddenly by a clammy mist, but the vehicle's automated voice booms as if in a children's fairy tale book, announcing the old names of the lonely stops where the ghosts gather: Crimsworth, Bedlam Road, Boundary Stone.

I alight at New Delight, an eighteenth-century stone terrace, crouched sheltering in a hillside cleft. Dusk is settling like the wings of a giant bird roosting. The sky is ashen with streaks of iridescent light. I'm reminded of the rays that are said to emanate from Will-o'-the-Wisp's lantern at night.

White bones of dried gorse snap. Gunfire beneath my shoes. Spongy terrain dictates my tilting gait as I balance precariously before finding firmer footing on a flagstone path leading up to the cottages.

Square eyes of electricity appear at the windows of number 6 as I approach. They dazzle like stage lighting. So much brighter than the stars which are mere pinpricks in a textile sky.

Henry opens the oak door before I have a chance to grasp the heavy iron knocker. As I had anticipated he is dressed smartly, in dark trousers and a grey shirt. I'm glad I made the effort to wear a dress and buy a decent bottle of red wine.

"Come in" Henry says, "I've done Käsespätzle."

I wonder if he's referring to a puppet character, but luckily I decide not to voice my thoughts.

The hallway is tiny and Henry, sensing my hesitation, flattens himself against the wall as I pass.

The living room is warm, the logs in the stove are glowing blaze-red, dancing orange. A small table is set for two by the mullion window. The candles are already lit and are melting into white stalactite forms.

The puppet theatre stands on a larger table pushed against the side wall. It is magnificent in glorious three-dimensional reality. Puppets are propped against it, their strings neatly laid out in parallel lines. There is a female marionette, her long blonde hair fastened back from her porcelain forehead by a golden coronet. An expression of sweet simplicity is painted on her smooth face. Her dress is turquoise, flashed with jade stripes, shimmering like a kingfisher in flight.

The male marionette is dressed in green jerkin and brown trousers. He carries a wooden sword, sewn onto his jerkin. His blue eyes stare above an aquiline nose. His pale pink mouth gapes open, articulated by fine threads attached to both sides of his square chin. Beside them one green frog squats, a miniature version of those I saw at the Handmade Parade gallery.

"We will eat first," Henry announces. "I'm more comfortable with cooking. Performance is controlled by the curtain call of chance, a play is always an unknown territory, the theatre of tomorrow where we are both audience and actor guessing the unturned page. I'll take your coat."

Henry disappears through a door at the back of the room, clutching my waterproof jacket like a hunting trophy.

I sit on one of the dining chairs, it seems safer, more structured than the sagging two-seater sofa.

Henry emerges from the kitchen with a white tea towel carefully folded over his left arm and a glinting cut-glass decanter sparkling liquid rubies. His hand trembles slightly as he pours the wine carefully into two pewter goblets.

"Käsespätzle is appropriate for tonight's entertainment," he says.

I wish he had just brought in the bottle, Maybe its label would have been more explanatory than Henry.

121

He places a green salad meticulously in the middle of the table, before returning with a bowl full of steaming pasta, topped with melted cheese and fried onion. He holds it like an offering to the gods.

"That looks good," I say, because it's obvious some response from me is required.

"I love macaroni cheese."

"It's Käsespätzle," Henry repeats with strenuous patience, "a dish from the southwestern region of Germany, Spätzle pasta. I'll just get the apple sauce."

The female marionette stares at me, her immobile mouth kept silent forever by her maker.

"They're organic, I picked them myself. Each a globe cupped in my hand, continents patinaed red by sun across smooth green seas."

It takes several seconds for me to surmise that Henry is referring to the main ingredient of the apple sauce, which he is bailing out of a gravy boat with a large spoon onto his plate.

"It's a shame you had to pulp them to make the sauce," I say, "but worth the carnage, shredded skin, smashed cores, scattered pips, because it looks delicious."

Henry thinks I'm serious.

"Spherical apothecaries," he responds, "essential for the metamorphosis of some wingless insects. It's no coincidence the apple was the forbidden fruit."

"How's the apple of your eye, the bear, getting on?" I ask, taking a big gulp of wine.

"Boris is almost complete. I've just got to work out his facial features tomorrow and then I'll be able to apply the finishing touches."

"I've got a Hansel and Gretel for dessert," Henry says gleefully, opening a shallow drawer under the dining table.

He carefully removes two little parcels wrapped in red gingham serviettes and places them onto a side plate.

"I was hoping to make a gingerbread house too; decorate it with striped candy and royal icing, but I've been too busy with the bear."

Henry puts the side plate next to me.

"Choose one, you've got a fifty percent chance of unwrapping the appropriate character."

My fingers fumble as I choose a parcel, so I concentrate on opening it carefully.

A golden-brown gingerbread woman emerges, headfirst. Her face is fixed in an iced smile. She has wavy lines of white icing at the bottom of her torso and across her shoulders, denoting a dress fastened by two blue smarties. She smells of ginger, sugar, and spice, but I don't want to eat her; to feel her limbs snap between my teeth.

"She's perfect," I say.

Henry smiles his approval and holds up his gingerbread Hansel, who is wearing iced lederhosen with green smartie buckles.

"Unmarried girls in Germany bake figures for good luck in finding love. They are distributed at fairs and the folklore is that the boy who eats their biscuit will marry them."

123

"The way to a man's heart is through his stomach."

I shock myself by repeating a dodgy mantra of my grandma's.

Henry ignores my remark.

"At the Roman festival of Saturnalia, culminating on our Christmas Day, human-shaped figurines were given as gifts; many of them edible. Saturn was their god of agriculture and time, and the custom may have echoed earlier ages when human sacrifices were made."

"I'd like to save mine."

I rapidly rewrap Gretel as Henry neatly beheads Hansel. He continues to crunch enthusiastically as he disappears behind the puppet theatre.

"Let the show begin."

The female marionette glides from the fly loft of the theatre, her turquoise gown floating gracefully, like a kingfisher's wing. She makes a smooth landing onto the centre of the stage, her strings taut.

Henry's voice is soft and melodic as he begins narrating.

"In a deep forest, a long time ago
where green light and ancient magic did glow
a princess with golden hair walked alone
her wild dandelion seed wishes all blown."

The princess' head swivels and somehow her enigmatic, placid face does appear sad. She raises a hand slowly to greet the male marionette who is clunking onto the stage. One of his strings becomes entangled in the wooden sword fastened onto the side of his green jerkin and I wonder if he is literally going to fall at her feet. The princess does not laugh, and neither do I. The dexterity of Henry's hands rescue the prince from such a potentially embarrassing entrance, and he comes to a jolting halt on the path just beyond where she is standing.

The prince's voice is silkier than his movements and his poetry.

"Enjoy the bluebells' chimes but be aware
in this dark, deep woodland lives a fierce bear.
Only I can protect you from danger
so greet me as a friend, not a stranger."

The princess raises her hands to her mouth, whether to stifle fear or a fit of giggling I'm not sure. The puppets embrace awkwardly, their wooden arms stiff. The princess plants an ungainly kiss on the ruddy cheek of the prince. There is a smell of scorched flesh and Henry yelps in pain as smoke billows from the deck of the stage. When the fog clears the prince has vanished and the frog puppet is jumping around the feet of a startled princess.

There is a long silence before I realise the play and pyrotechnics are over, and Henry is waiting for applause. I clap and he emerges from behind the theatre bowing deeply.

"I'm a puppeteer not in control of the strings," he says shuffling his feet. "This is the way of modern magic, a princess thinks she's kissing a prince and then he turns into a frog, not always immediately in a flash of flame, often he crawls slowly out of the smoke. But sometimes there is a sort of happy ever after. What I'm trying to say is, accept me, warts and all. Sorry I'm mixing my metaphors, toads have bumpy skins, frogs are

125

smooth, and I'd like to give it a go with you. Have a relationship I mean."

I decide to grasp the strings firmly in my hands.

"Create me a female marionette with a moving mouth who can speak, and maybe then I'll say yes."

The Crystal

by Janet Griffiths

She pulled the loft ladder down and climbed up it, pulling her hefty body weight up with her. She disappeared for what seemed like a long time but probably wasn't.

When she emerged, she had an old carved wooden box in her hand. She placed it on a shelf and prepared the table in front of us, placing a dark-red chenille tablecloth on top. She smoothed out all the wrinkles until she was satisfied with its appearance and then fetched an old black book, blew away the dust and cobwebs and cleaned the outside with her hands.

She rustled through the pages until she came to the one she wanted.

"Ah" a long sigh emerged from the depths of her being.

I wondered what she was 'ahing' about. She closed her eyes and beckoned to me to do the same. When her eyes eventually opened, they were shining. Light was literally pouring out of them. The light grew brighter and brighter and everything in the room began to shake, quietly at first, then louder and louder. Objects were jumping up and down.

As I watched, first a feather, then a glass goblet, a shoe, some flowers, an old photograph in a silver frame and lastly, a candle jumped on to the table.

The table was shaking and jumping around, and all the objects danced round each other. Everything in the room was shaking and rattling.

She ran her hands over the table three times in a clockwise direction and the objects quietened down and everything else in the room came to rest.

She placed the candle in the middle of the table, lit it, sat back in her chair again and closed her eyes. Her breath became deeper and deeper, hoarse-like, almost like it was difficult to breathe.

Outside, an owl hooted three times. I wondered if this was a sign.

She took the old wooden box down from the shelf and opened the lid. Inside was a beautiful dark green egg-shaped stone.

She held the stone in her hands, and it started to glow. Little rays of light circled round it, and it began to spin. It spun round and round in her hands faster and faster then jumped into the air and landed in my lap.

I looked down and she beckoned to me to pick it up. I held it in my hands passing it from one to the other. It was getting hotter. The pale green patterns ingrained in it moved round and round the outside chasing each other. It was hot, almost too hot to touch, but I knew I had to keep holding it.

Suddenly it jumped out of my hands and into the middle of the table, almost extinguishing the candle. The glowing grew fainter and fainter until it came to rest.

She consulted the book again, took a piece of chalk from the shelf and drew a hexagon on the tabletop. The feather, glass goblet, shoe, flowers and the old photograph in the silver frame all moved into position on the corners of the hexagon. The candle moved into the middle.

Outside, the owl hooted three times again.

She tore three pieces of paper from a sheet, handed them to me with a pen and told me to write. I wasn't sure what I should be writing so I closed my eyes and pondered. Eventually I wrote each of my secret wishes on the pieces and handed them back to her.

I waited with bated breath. Was this the end of all my dreams, or just the beginning?

Heartsease

by Alison Milner

"Come meet me on the moors," he said, his eyes bright reflecting sunlight.

"We'll breathe peat, drink dew. Lay in the moss and grass, until our feelings pass."

So Anne did. But they didn't, the feelings I mean.

Now there is nowhere for Anne to hide within the lines of her diary, and nothing more to be found. Only constant seeking.

They had circled each other for a week. He a full moon. She a wolf with a lolling tongue which would not stiffen to shape the words she feared to speak.

Then a confluence. Anne's heart naked before his eyes, his emotions streaming fanciful notions. Their kisses punctuated their prose, typed their one-act drama. A Midas sun burned their lives gold, before night spread across the valley like a black ink stain.

The darkness blossomed chrysanthemum lips, a flowering wreath of silent longing in Anne's garden. A solitary Halloween rose, petals torn, reached for a winter dawn.

Maybe Anne was in search of lost time. She was aware of travelling west, towards a setting sun.

"We all are," she thought, "even him."

He was not hiding, not seeking, not really even pursuing. He hunted like a heron patiently waiting for prey, watching the river run past, sensing the rhythms of the sea; smelling salt and an iron tang of blood. In full flight he glided, feathered her in soft charm, and she sheltered beneath his great wingspan.

They'd first met in a busy café. He had punctured her space, sitting down in the vacant chair opposite.

"You don't mind, do you?" It wasn't a question.

"I've always wanted to be an artist," his voice gushed like the coffee steaming from the metal teats of the machine behind the counter. "But I can't express myself in images, naturalistic, illustrative or abstract. That's why I try and create my pictures in writing."

"I write too," Anne confessed, "mostly my diary."

"Have you seen the new exhibition at the art gallery?" He was obviously more intent on talking.

Funnily enough, Anne had just spent over an hour there. She couldn't recollect seeing him in the spaces between the pictures, but he was vaguely familiar. She whispered that she'd found the etched patterns in the sketching tactile; the dots and dashes reminding her of morse code.

"Or a kind of braille," he said, "the reaching of an understanding through touch.

"I'd like to read your writing and share some of mine with you. You could come round to my house one evening?"

Anne twisted the ring on her little finger, it felt tight on her hot hand.

"A coffee then," he smiled, "with cake, on Monday morning in Penguin Café at 11.00?"

"Yes," Anne said. A short word, one syllable.

For decades Monday mornings had been bleak affairs for Anne. Even the sugar in strong coffee couldn't sweeten the day, or drug her through the tedium, or stop the work worm gnawing.

Recently, on most Monday mornings he had offered her Darjeeling tea on a flowered tray and exquisite chocolates from a richly decorated box. He played her mind like a harp, plucking poetry like the notes of a melody. He became the conductor of Anne's orchestra, the figure etched in charcoal on the internal landscapes of her brain.

That October, they had baptised their relationship in an amber waterfall, drunk on heady peat and cloying love. A clay loam from which they created themselves as a couple, in the bitter, goose-pimpled cold.

Anne couldn't stop inhaling him. Once they visited the sea together, a wide estuary where time paints grains of existence. Salt spray stung her lips. A biro line of blue underscored their horizon, blurring sky and ocean; framing sand palettes, beige to brown, in darkening stripes.

The path across the pale expanse of beach was marked by red danger signs and green myrtle branches. Only the hard ridges of mud-ripples beneath their boots suggested a tide retreated. They waded through stars, gleaming on water trapped in deep ebb.

He said he would carve their love in lines of poetry on the shoreline rocks. He hadn't brought a chisel, so they settled on scrawling their promises in the sand; only to then watch their vows vanish in flotsam and foam.

"Remember me to the sea, every time you visit her," Anne said, but his heart pounded only blood.

Anne didn't understand why reality is often described as cold or hard. Her reality is wet and soft; winter rain, days of drenching drizzle. The millstone grit sucking the damp like a greedy child at a mother's breast. Moisture staining chimney hearths and hearts.

Anne shed her skin for him, ingesting his heavy magic, but it proved venomous. Their snake fire coiled cold, rotting in the leaf mould of a dead season. His passion dried with the air, leaving her brittle with neglect.

That first winter without him, stark trees were engraved black on a misty canvas, their bare twigs clutching a grey sky. Anne's darkness melted gradually as the light brightened, and the season walked beside her towards spring. She began to notice green shoots, origami wrapped, piercing the cloak of dead leaves layered in the woods at Hardcastle Crags. Anne's hiking stretched as the days lengthened. Her strides became stronger and her confidence in summer's return grew, echoing the birdsong.

In time, the shoots sprouted angular stems, branching out, a miniature version of the tall trees looming above them. A posy of flowers blossomed, tints of yellow, purple, and white on each tiny petal, and she recognised Love-Lies-Bleeding, Heartsease, Love-in-Idleness, Call-me-to-you. So many names for such a little Wild Pansy.

Anne observed the flowers protecting themselves from rain by dropping their heads in wet weather, shielding their delicate faces from the tears of water. She read about the medicinal properties of Heartsease in Turner's *Herbal*, how Northern people in Anglo-Saxon Britain called it 'thys herbe Banwurt because it helpeth bones to knyt againe' and in later centuries, Herbal Trinitatis, a dedication to the Trinity, as every bloom is blessed with three colours.

Anne picked a handful of Heartsease at dawn on the Summer Solstice. Not for its potency as a love charm, she no longer dreamt of romance on midsummer nights, but for its power in healing afflictions of the heart.

Shining Light

by Roy Greenwood

Old Arthur had been wrong. Joe knew it, but it had been a good argument. A few pints and a chat in the pub was a pleasant way of spending an evening. The company had been good, even though the brown liquid which passed for beer had little to recommend it – but as many people had remarked: "At least you can drink it, not like the water."

The chill night air hit Joe with sledgehammer force as he emerged from the hot noisy atmosphere of the pub. The hazy halo of his cigarette smoke which curled about his head vanished as an icy breeze blew down the valley.

Joe left the roadway that wound snake-like parallel to the river and picked his way carefully over the hillside. He knew this area like his own front room and had been picking his way back to his isolated home from the pub two miles away for more years than he cared to remember.

He paused to reflect. He remembered his childhood. He remembered those rolling hillsides stretching almost as far as you could see. Now the gods of concrete and metal were fast demanding their ever increasing homage.

He looked down from the top of the slope at the myriad of lights, more numerous than raisins in a Christmas cake, which surrounded the now few remaining miles of open countryside he regarded as home.

He glanced at the flickering horizon and the flashing headlights of traffic on the motorway as it cut across the top of the hillside with ruler perfection as though some giant hand had sliced off the hilltop with a huge scimitar.

Below him stretched the river. The reflection of the lights in the fast-moving water gave it a pleasant but hypnotic appearance, only the darkness disguising the poisonous foul-looking liquid which gurgled between the dying banks.

Joe shivered and shook his head as if to shatter the image. Joe Finney was not the brightest, but he was happy in his own little rut.

Each day he had to venture down into that world of concrete, metal and glass that called itself the city, but he could return to his few square miles of countryside. He glanced at the luminous dial of his watch and shivered again.

Better get moving he thought and, still smiling at old Arthur's remarks, he set off along the path which forced its way over the hillside, along the awesome sentinels carrying the overhead power lines with a humming like the wings of some giant insect.

He looked up at the pylon, towering, forbidding and spider-like above him, silhouetted eerily against the night sky.

Staring zombie-like at the pylon, he walked along and then suddenly stumbled.

"Shit," he cursed as he wrenched his ankle and fell heavily.

Wincing he sat up and started to rub his ankle. He looked at the ground around his feet and then over his shoulder. It was particularly flat at this point and he could see nothing which could have caused his fall.

He turned back and there at his feet lay a shining, silvery, crystal-like sphere about the size of a cricket ball.

"How could I have missed that bloody thing," he said out loud, unable to believe his eyes.

He stared. He could not tear his eyes away. Some hypnotic force gripped them and would not let go.

The pain in his ankle seemed to vanish as he gradually got to his knees.

"Oh my God, what is it?"

The words tumbled from his lips, but he sensed rather than heard them. Then slowly involuntarily he reached out for the sphere.

His eyes were still fixed on the shining object as its light now came in a pulsating rhythm. His mind whirled as his hands slowly came together around the sphere. They seemed to have a will of their own, he had no control over them. His eyes were fixed rigidly on the sphere as everything else blotted out.

He could no longer see the mass of lights which was the ever-growing city, or the winding river or even the pylon brooding over him. His mind fought for control, but lost. He started to get up still holding the sphere. It was as though he was standing back watching himself. He could do nothing about it. His eyes were still fixed on the shining light in his hands.

In a trance-like state, he stood there, unblinking eyes staring at the sphere. Gradually he felt himself falling ever inwards, like someone leaning over a high cliff and being drawn down towards the pounding surf. But Joe could not hold back, he was falling ever deeper and deeper into the light, whirling round and round as he became the light until slowly its brightness began to fade and there was nothing but a grey swirling mist.

Again Joe could sense the mist rather than feel it. He could sense himself. Something weird had happened, but at least he was still alive – or was he?

Slowly, the mist began to clear and a strange new environment opened around him. Gone were the hillside and the city lights and in their place row upon row of box-like constructions stretching as far as he could see.

Overhead, gone too was the silvery moonlight and the friendly familiar stars. Instead all he could see was a sky the colour of lead and a sun which looked more like a dying ember than a life-giving burst of energy.

Again he had the strange feeling. He sensed his surroundings, himself and his own immobility. He was a spectator, the scene having been set, he was waiting for the action. What that would be, he could not even guess. He did not know where he was or whether he even still existed.

Suddenly his eyes moved. Again it was an involuntary action to which he merely had to submit. They moved from side to side, then focused like a camera's zoom lens on the boxes.

As his eyes adjusted to the sudden close-up, Finney became aware of the dimensions. The boxes appeared to be about eight feet square and seemed to be made of glass within a metal framework. Inside each box was a lonely figure. He sensed the figures were struggling, struggling to escape. Each one looked the same, wearing drab brown clothes, the same hair – everything.

The nearest figure turned towards him, a look of pleading and desperation on its face – an expression of a soul in hell, crying out for help. He gazed into the wild, but somehow strangely familiar eyes. Then the next figure turned to face him and he saw that same expression and those same wild eyes. When the third figure turned he started to scream and was still screaming as his own face turned towards him for the fourth time and the mist once again enclosed him.

As the city lights and the stars of his world returned, Joe Finney was still screaming, his eyes now blinded by the shining light in his hands. He started to run, stumbling in his shining blindness, his eyes held nothing now except the explosion of searing light and memory of what he had seen, experienced, felt or dreamed. His mind was like a shattered mosaic, too shaken to form any judgement.

Like a drunken man he stumbled along. With the light in his eyes he never saw the small gulley until his foot suddenly connected with mid-air and he tumbled, arms and legs flailing like a used scarecrow, on to the rocky outcrop below.

With a thud, life was knocked out of him and the body that had once been Joe Finney rolled to the bottom of the gully leaving a trail of red trickling down into the ever-growing pool of blood that spread from the battered head.

As his head hit the rock, Finney's hand had opened, and the shining light had been hurled across the gulley like a comet blazing across the night sky. It hit the opposite slope and bounced down on to the rocks to shatter like a Roman candle in

139

a shower of brightness. The thousands of tiny fragments lay there sparkling like a swarm of fireflies until gradually their light faded and the gulley and its bloody contents were again shrouded in darkness.

The man in the first box sank to his knees, hands clasping his forehead. For some seconds he knelt there swaying from side to side at the pain in his head and then fell with a thud against the wall.

"Well?" came an anxious voice from the next box.

The man still clasping his head did not answer.

"What happened?" asked the voice in a more anxious tone.

Slowly the man took his hands from his forehead and with eyes closed and chin on chest, he replied, "He's dead."

"Dead....dead," repeated the voice, "Oh no. But what about your crystal ball?"

"Gone....shattered....destroyed," replied the kneeling man, now staring at the grid which linked his box with the life supporting and dominating connection to the computer brain.

He heard sobbing coming through the wall amplification.

"The only hope gone," came the jerky voice, "God help us now."

"It's even too late for him," replied the kneeling man. "God's a different shape now," he mumbled, staring at the grid.

Second Skin

by Janet Griffiths

Her skin was old, wrinkly and crepey. Full of sunspots, moles and freckles. It was skin that belonged to a woman who had lived a long time.

That was the skin she showed to the world, or actually, apart from her hands and face, she covered it up.

But she had a secret. She had a second skin, a skin she brought out at night when she was all alone. She would slither her way into it, pulling it tight over the body, concealing all her flaws.

Her second skin took years off her. She liked to walk around her house naked in it, admiring herself in the mirrors.

After a period of nakedness, she would dress herself in the tiniest, slinkiest little dresses and dance, barefoot, tossing her hair down her back, eyes sparkling, laughing and singing to herself.

Tonight was a full moon. She looked out of her bedroom window and there it was, a bright luminous moon shining out of a clear dark sky, surrounded by stars and constellations.

She opened her back door and tentatively stepped outside on to the back lawn. There were no lights in either of the neighbour's houses. Good, they must be in bed.

She started humming to herself, her favourite tune, a Mantovani favourite. The grass was faintly dewy, it felt delightful on her feet as she started to dance, slowly at first, her body swaying as if in a trance, then her feet started to move in bigger and bigger steps.

Dancing from one side of the lawn to the other, round and round she went. Her second skin gleamed in the moonlight, she caught sight of her reflection in her pond and admired herself.

Her feet went faster and faster, round and round they went, swirling and twirling, faster and faster and faster.

Her heart began pounding in her chest. She was finding it hard to breathe, she had palpitations.

She started to feel worried, but alas she couldn't stop dancing. Faster and faster and faster. She tried to breath deeper, *breathe from the belly,* she told herself, but she couldn't.

The Last Angel of Skaði

by Chris Freeman

As the four cavers ventured ever further into the limestone labyrinth they were conscious of the fact that no man had ever set foot in this unexplored cave before. Now, after nearly five hours of crawling through tiny passages, their leader, James, came into a huge underground cathedral of such magnificence, that he was almost overwhelmed by its beauty. His headlamp lit up the scene as though it were a searchlight to another world.

Mark was next to break out into the opening, followed by Sarah, who couldn't believe her eyes when her lamp first picked out the sheer size of the cavern. Her light seemed to go on forever and in the distance, picked out a small waterfall, tumbling down over the sparkling limestone. Down below them was a small lake, inky black in the half light of the headlamps. Sarah called back to George, their photographer, to hurry to bring up the equipment that would allow them to capture forever, the scene on camera. George, who was somewhat plumper than the others, struggled through the small opening into the cave.

"Oh thanks for the help there folks," he said, but his words were lost in the vastness of the scene and his voice tailed of into a whisper as he drew in his breath and suddenly exclaimed – "WOW! I've seen some caverns in my time, but this is awesome!"

George quickly set up the equipment to record the sheer magnitude of this wonderful cavern. Truly this was what made lugging that equipment for hours all worthwhile. Mind you, lugging equipment had got a whole lot easier thanks to digital photography, working with lightweight lithium batteries and LED lights, compared to lead acid batteries and tungsten lamps. Even so, poor old George had a real sweat on, but for him, this was what it was all about. The sheer grandeur of it all and knowing that they were the first ever to witness this magnificent scene made the journey well worth the effort.

Sarah had managed to get down to the water's edge and half walked, half swum, to the other side and had clambered up the slippery limestone face on the other side. George shouted to her to stay there and train her headlamp up to the cave's ceiling, some 30 feet above them, so that he could capture the whole scene on camera and use her figure for scale.

Sarah stood motionless as George prepared to make the shot, with her headlight pointed up to illuminate the green fluorescence of the cavern's ceiling.

'Green,' she thought, 'isn't that strange, because one associates green with the living world, and here were are, hundreds of feet below ground, and we still see the colour green.'

"5, 4, 3, 2, 1 – GOT IT!" called George, "That's a great shot!"

"AIR," exclaimed Sarah, "AIR."

James and Mark came up alongside Sarah and looked at her.

"What do you mean, AIR?" said James.

"AIR!" exclaimed Sarah, "AIR! I can feel air!"

They all stood motionless, heads up as if feeling for something and then they all felt it. The faintest of draughts on their cheeks.

Looking round they could see just the tiniest of holes in the rock face and Sarah suddenly had a brainwave.

"Turn off your lights!" she screamed, "Turn off your lights! There's green here and there shouldn't be any at all underground."

They dutifully did what Sarah had asked and sure enough, after several minutes to allow their eyes to accustom to the total darkness, the small hole began to glimmer with light in the dark of the rock surrounding it.

James came forward and sniffed at the hole.

"I can definitely smell fresh air," he said, "but how we get through to it heaven alone knows. It could take a week to break out a hole big enough for a person to crawl through."

He looked at his watch.

"Out of time folks," he said, "We can come back tomorrow, now that we know there's something worth coming back for and we can bring some tunnelling equipment to try to break through to wherever that air is coming from."

"Oh joy!" exclaimed George scornfully, "More bloody kit to lug! Thanks for nothing, I'm sure!"

The four-man surface crew were glad to finally get a radio signal that the cave party were close to emerging and they could soon be hauled back up to safety.

Fast forward two weeks and the whole party were back on scene with all of the equipment that they thought they might need underground to pick their way through to the air source.

George, still with his photographic kit, politely declined to assist with the mining equipment, or the food.

The food was to allow them to stay underground for several days, thus allowing for a concerted effort to break through the rock face and they needed it, too.

James, leader of the expedition, was first to start hacking away at the soft limestone and after 30 minutes handed over to Mark, who was the strongman of the act and stayed at the job for nearly an hour, declining all offers of assistance. Sarah took her turn and did what she could, but was glad when James stepped up again.

"George!" he called, "What about you?"

"Still filming," called George and stayed firmly put behind his cameras – and the working party.

Time has little meaning underground and it was well into the third day that James realised they were fast running out of time, but they were so near to breaking through that he decided to take a straw poll of whether they should stay a bit longer than planned. They all agreed that they should battle on, as they seemed to be so close to their target.

Sarah stepped up for what she hoped was her last stint and was just getting to the point of exhaustion when the whole rock face in front of her collapsed and dropped away. Her heart almost stopped for a moment at the shock of what she had accomplished and there it was, an almost perfect inverted U-shaped tunnel. Slowly, and very carefully, she clambered over the fallen rock to enter the tunnel, which was some 9 feet high and maybe 4 feet wide. It was perfect, as if it had been worked by some wonderful machine that could tunnel this shape, with perfectly smooth sides. As the others came forwards, they all stood and looked in awe at the symmetry of the tunnel.

"Lava tube," said Mark, "This must be a lava tube."

"In limestone?" queried Sarah.

Mark, who was a bit of a geologist explained that the fault line earthquake that had caused the vast plain area to sink and leave a huge cliff, may well have triggered a volcanic eruption. The earthquake must have been massive to cause the land to sink nearly 100 feet and that they must be somewhere about halfway up that cliff in this lava tunnel.

James now took the lead again as they walked forward into the ever-widening tunnel, with the light and air draught becoming stronger by the moment.

The lava tube was far from straight and after several long bends they began to emerge into the beginning of an old limestone cave. As the light became stronger, James' radio crackled and he stopped to check the signal.

"I'll radio up to surface now," he called, "and let them know where we are."

As he called the surface crew he walked forward and just as they answered he stopped dead in his tracks.

"My God!" he exclaimed.

"You okay?" came the radio reply.

"There's a woman strung up in here," replied James.

In the half-light coming in from the tree-lined cave entrance, James could see that the woman, who looked to be about 30, was slim and clothed in tattered shreds that hung from her lithe body. Her arms were high above her head, pulled taught into a 'Y' shape. There were what looked like straw ropes around her wrists, but her fingers strangely gripped the rope above her hands, almost as if seeking to alleviate the strain on her wrists. The ropes were passed over protrusions in the rock above her and she hung there motionless with her feet some way off the ground.

James called to the others to give him a lift up, so that he could cut the poor woman free and with quite a stretch he just managed to cut the ropes and the woman fell into the arms of George, who had stepped up to be just in the right place. George, not expecting the woman to have been so heavy, almost collapsed with the weight.

Sarah, who was the medic of the group, looked at this strange body. Obviously, from the disintegrated clothing, the poor woman must have been dead for years, yet her body wasn't desiccated, as it should have been. She instinctively felt for a pulse, but knew that she would find none. James, ever the gentleman, took of his heavy caving jacket and placed it over the woman.

James radioed up to the surface crew that they would need a stretcher to lift the woman out of the cave and up to the surface, which was only some 30 feet above the roof of the cave entrance. They hacked away some of the vegetation that covered the cave entrance and slowly manoeuvred the stretcher, with its gruesome load, out of the cave.

Once the stretcher was at the surface, a rope ladder was dropped down and one by one the cave team made their way to the top of the cliff face.

Now the whole eight strong team pondered over how the woman came to be down there and how she had been put there and by whom and for what purpose. And none of them could even think to explain her lack of desiccation. They had no communication with the outside world here and it would be another two-day hike before they could get into radio contact with anyone. The enigma was theirs.

As night was falling, they decided that the best option was to stay put for the night and make camp there; as the weather was still warm and dry, the lightweight tents would well suffice their needs. Tired and much in need of rest, it wasn't long before the whole camp was silent.

Sarah, always the light sleeper was first to awaken at first light, to the sound of what she could only describe as some strange foreign, maybe Scandinavian, or Gallic female voice, singing lightly in the background. She couldn't imagine that any of the men would have such a high pitch, and so sweet too. She was the only woman in the party and a shiver ran down her spine at the thought of what she might see when she crawled out of her tent.

There, dressed in James' mauve caving jacket was the woman, sat next to a roaring fire watching for the kettle to boil. Without looking round she bade Sarah a good morning and would she like a brew of tea. Sarah was dumbstruck. The woman was dead. She had seen it for herself. She must have been hanging up in that cave for years for her clothes to have rotted like that, yet here she was, large as life and twice as cheerful. Even the vegetation at the mouth of the cave would have taken many years to grow across like it had and it was undisturbed when they cut it back to get out.

"Don't be afraid of me, please," said the lady, "Just accept that I am here now with you, my rescuers. You have done your good deed and I am grateful. Would you like milk and sugar with your tea?"

"Er – No thanks," said Sarah, still shocked by what she was witnessing. "I like mine black, but not too strong."

The voices had stirred the others, who, one by one, emerged slowly from their tents to witness this miracle.

Once everyone was assembled the lady bade them all to sit and take tea with her whilst she explained everything.

Her mission was to be anywhere where she was most needed and it was the problems of the local tribe that had brought her here from afar. Even as she tried to help the people, there were those amongst them who were against her, for they sought to ally themselves to their oppressors to further their own ends. It was they who had strung her up in the cave for it was their belief that the shape of the 'Y' was their way to rid themselves of her powers. They knew of the earthquake and of the volcanic eruption that followed and knew of the cave and old lava tube. They hoped that the volcano would return and engulf her in that cave, for it was only the fire of the earth than could destroy her.

In their turn the local tribe was engulfed by the tribe that they had sought to join forces with, and they in turn had succumbed to their neighbours, who in their turn had slowly been exterminated by the diseases of the foreign invaders from

Europe. So now, no one inhabited the wild plains, or the high cliffs and she was left to rot in the cave. Waiting for her rescuers.

"Can I please keep this coat, James?" she asked as she stood up.

"Er, yes – I suppose so," stammered James and with that she turned to leave.

"But who are you and where are you from?" called Sarah as the lady began to drift skywards and fade away.

"Why, I'm the last Angel of Skaði. I have no home, but you might call for me at Dunvegan," she said as she faded from view.

Only a Tram Ride Away

by Joan Watson

Agnes shivered, pulled her coat tightly around her and gently closing the gate behind her with a click, hurried up the back lane.

"I've made my decision," she thought, "I'm not going back now."

A faint light appeared in the dark sky as she stumbled against a dustbin with a crash. The cry of a baby started up in one of the narrow houses and her footsteps echoed eerily on the black cobbles as she turned into Hilton Road. Hurrying along past the pawnbroker and the pub, she thought of Michael and Mary Edith asleep in their cot.

"Please God, don't let them wake up before I get back," she whispered to herself.

Outside the corner shop, its small window dusty with empty packets of Rinso, Dolly Blue and piles of scrubbing bushes, the tram waited patiently for its first passengers of the day. Under the yellow lamp the conductor stamped his cold feet on the frozen ground as he chatted to the driver. Agnes quickened her pace and carefully climbed the steps on board. Sitting down on one of the long, slatted wooden benches that faced each other, she looked around her. Two workmen, half asleep, glanced up and then huddled back into their coats, pulling their caps down over their eyes. She heard the sharp rasping cough of the driver

152

on the second fag of the day, as in the distance the early morning hooters of the shipyards wailed.

Jumping up the steps the conductor shouted, "Right Bobby, ready when you are."

The tram slowly jerked and clanged into action as the driver turned the handle and they set off through the empty streets.

Agnes sat quite still, only gently swaying from side to side as the tram made its way through the narrow streets of cottages and terraced houses. The conductor seeing the solitary working class woman sitting there alone, paused for his fare.

"Fares please." he said.

"How much to Hendon?" she asked looking up at him

"Ha'penny to you," he smiled, punching the ticket with a ping.

"My, you're up early, pet."

Half smiling in return, she made no reply. Placing the ticket carefully in her pocket, she returned to gazing out the window. The sky was lighter now and streaked with pale pink as she allowed her mind to wander off in a daydream. Pictures slid through her mind but were quickly pushed back into their box. She never allowed herself to remember. By keeping busy all day, she would fall into a deep sleep at night, tired out.

The conductor, having returned to his post on the platform, studied the woman with interest. He saw a slight figure of about thirty years of age, dressed in a dark blue skirt under an old brown coat. A pair of buttoned boots could be seen under her skirts, worn with age and vigorous polishing. Sitting upright on the bench, her long, strong hands lay in her lap.

"She's no beauty," he thought.

Her hair, obviously her best feature being auburn and wavy was tied back tightly in a bun at the nape of her neck. A stern face with pronounced cheek bones and a bony nose was set off by a small, firm chin. When she had half smiled he noticed that her blue eyes sparkled, turning her face into a pretty one for a moment.

"What is she up to? No good, I'll be bound."

Agnes was aware of the conductor's curiosity, but her mind was on more important things.

"I'll go straight in and ask to see him if he refuses to see me."

She wouldn't countenance that. One of the men stood up from his seat and swayed down the aisle.

"Next stop," he shouted, and then pausing beside Agnes said, "Agnes Doherty isn't it? How are you? How's your Michael? I heard he joined up. Give him my regards when you next write. Billy Burns is the name. I worked with him at the Gas Company."

Agnes smiled and nodded and then he was gone, jumping off the tram as it slowed down at the next stop.

"Hendon," shouted the conductor, and Agnes found herself standing on the pavement, the damp, salty air reviving her, curling the wisps of hair around her face. With her head held high she walked determinedly towards the munitions factory.

The gateman stopped her in her tracks,

"Hold on a minute, pet," he shouted, "You can't go through there."

154

She turned and smiled,

"Mr Briggs knows me well. I just want a quick word with him."

The gateman, a small fussy man finally found a lad to take her to the offices and she picked her way gingerly over the uneven ground to the staircase. The noise and smell from the factory surrounded her and she was deposited on a bench outside a large glass door and told to wait.

Agnes was staring to feel tired now. Her nervous energy was gradually leaving her as she settled back on the bench in the dusty corridor.

"Why am I doing this mad thing?"

She could not explain why, even to herself.

"I know what my neighbours and family would say, but I've never let anyone's opinion change mine. All I know is that I have to be independent of Michael. He could die in the war or be badly injured and I want to give the two children the best start in life."

Rehearsing her speech to Sammy Briggs, she hoped desperately that he would remember her.

Voices could be heard behind the glass door, so taking her hanky she quickly wiped over her boots. As she pushed the whisps of hair of her face the door opened and a young, well-dressed woman appeared, ushering her into the office and asking her name as they went in.

Agnes stood in the doorway and quickly glanced round the room. The woman told her to sit down and disappeared through a doorway on the left. A huge carved wooden desk stood in front of the window.

A coal fire roared away in the fireplace. After a few minutes a red-faced man of about forty years of age entered the room. He wore a smart suit with a fancy waistcoat and a gold watch and chain. Sitting down at his desk he started talking at great speed about how there was no overtime, no jobs for women and then looking up, he stared at Agnes.

"I know you from somewhere, don't I?" he said slowly.

Agnes smiled. "Yes Sammy, you do. If I tell you my maiden name was Sullivan and I worked for your mam..."

"Goodness gracious me," he interrupted at once, "of course I remember you, Agnes. What would we have done without you I'll never know. How are you?"

Agnes settled back in her chair and told him her tale. How angry she had been when Michael left to take the King's shilling, how she was determined to work hard to support herself and the two bairns and how she had had a brilliant idea.

As Agnes talked, Sam Briggs half listened and half remembered. Agnes had worked for his mother as housekeeper, cook and scullery maid all rolled into one. She had been highly thought of by his mother as a hard worker and a good friend. When his mother had been taken ill she had been a marvellous nurse as well. He had found out after her death that Agnes had received a letter from the hospital to train to become a nurse but had turned down the opportunity to stay with the family. He owed her a great deal, but she would never hear of extra money and hated praise. Anything he could do for her he would.

"Well Agnes, what is this marvellous idea of yours? Keep it short though, I've been up all night," he said with a smile.

"Everyday for a month now I have been coming at dinner time with our Edith, my daughter, to sell sandwiches at your factory gates. I have made some money, but it is very exasperating as I can only sell one basketful. I would like to rent the small wooden hut just by the gates. It's empty and I could turn it into kiosk in no time. Then I could buy ingredients and make up the sandwiches on the spot."

She stopped talking and waited. She was not going to beg, but she had her heart set on this.

Sam shook his head. "I'm sorry Agnes, but that hut is to be pulled down next month so that we can widen the road. If there was anything I could do, I would."

Agnes stood up straight away, smoothed her coat front and said her goodbyes. Biting back the tears she made her way to the gate and then on to the tram stop. Sitting on the tram, she thought about what had happened.

"I never thought for one minute he would refuse me for whatever reason."

By the time she reached the stop she had recovered and was determined to think of another plan.

Meanwhile Sam Briggs sat for a while thinking hard and then called his secretary to take a letter.

Thursday was pay day and therefore Friday was rent day. Agnes always had it ready, with the rent book, on top of the hall cupboard. Down the street back doors could be heard slamming shut as hard-up folks either rushed off with their children for a hasty visit to Grandma's or hurried quickly to the pawn shop. Soon after ten o'clock, Bill Teasdale knocked at the door and Agnes picked up the money and rent book as she opened the front door.

"Morning Mrs Doherty, money ready as usual I see."

Agnes smiled and handed it over.

"How's your wife Bill, has she recovered properly from the 'flu?"

"Much better now, thanks."

He turned away to go, and then, remembering something stopped.

"Oh, remember you asked me about renting a house with a shop? Well there's a lovely one with four bedrooms on the corner of Shepherd Street in Millfield. Just come up for rent."

Agnes shook her head sadly, "Bill, I couldn't afford the rent for that sort of property."

"Oh I think you can, it's only eleven shillings a week."

Agnes gasped. Her mind worked overtime as she realised that with her savings she could just afford it. It was a dream come true.

"Yes, I'll take it. Thank you."

Bill Teasdale went on to the next house.

"It's very puzzling," he thought, "That sort of property has a long waiting list and the rent should be at least five shillings more than it is."

He looked at the letter in his hands.

"There's no doubt about it. Still, Sam Briggs, the new landlord, must know what he's doing."

As soon as he'd gone, Agnes grabbed Edith and rushed out of the back gate and round to Rose, her sister-in -law, to tell her the good news. Rose was delighted for her at first until she thought about it more carefully.

"But Agnes, it's such a long way, we'll never see you," she sighed.

"Rose," laughed Agnes, "it's only a tram ride away."